HE OPENED HIS MOUTH to laugh, showing his rows of gleaming fangs. Medb would never forget that laugh, so full of slow, heinous triumph.

The monster rode closer to her father. The two Fomors holding Aed stepped aside, leaving the King of the Sligo to stand alone. To his credit, he disdained to look at the beast before him, and instead looked at his daughter.

"Medb, it rests with you."

Those were his last words, for even as Medb opened her mouth to scream, "Run, Father!" Balor leaned forward in his saddle and opened his demonic eye. A painful, searing shaft of light struck Aed, who crumpled under its blast. He slumped to the ground like a suddenly emptied sack. His skin shriveled and darkened, stretching over the bones of his face to uncover a ghastly grin of teeth. His eyes sank into a pair of vacant pits staring sightlessly through scorched, leathery lids. His body withered to an unrecognizable shape with hands shriveled into claws.

When the notorious King of the Fomors shut his evil eye and straightened, he gestured to one of his brutes. "Bring me his head; I want it for my collection."

CELTIC TALES™
BALOR OF THE EVIL EYE

Celtic Tales™

Balor of the Evil Eye

Nadine Crenshaw

Prima Publishing

ISBN: 0-7615-0247-5
Library of Congress Catalog Card Number: 95-71554
Printed in the United States of America
96 97 98 99 EE 10 9 8 7 6 5 4 3 2 1

ACKNOWLEDGMENTS

I must admit that without Ron Wartow's previous Prima book, *Celtic Tales: Balor of the Evil Eye–The Official Strategy Guide*, I could not have written this novel.

Also, many thanks to the patience and assistance of Mark Hughes of Koei Corporation.

Dedicated to the wide-angled vision and ready laughter of Paula Munier Lee.

Long and since when first he came
With his foul lot, this devil bane
A murderous gaze, his awful fame
On crimson fields, our heroes slain.

Winter winds bring with them sorrow
That curséd day our two worlds wed
A brighter day we pray the morrow
A child stolen, a Fomor fed!

Days of yore, brave race we were
Hearty steeds and men of valor
Now huddled round like frightened curs
Oh, who will face the mighty Balor?

The Chief Characters of *Celtic Tales: Balor of the Evil Eye*

A note on Celtic pronunciation: In general, mh and bh are sounded as *v*; ch is breathed *k*, as in the familiar lo*ch*; -gach is the sound of a hard -*gy*; and the profusion of vowels is usually a single sound.

Aed King of the Sligo tribe, Medb's father
Ainle A young warrior under Medb's rule
Arawn A wandering warrior recruited to Medb's service
Balor of the Evil Eye Lord of Darkness, master of the Fomors
Bran A young Druid under Medb's rule
Caipre A bard, Medb's delegate in Clifden
Catabadh A Druid priest under Medb's rule
Conann Balor's lieutenant
Ceridwen The Archdruid of Eire, a prophetess
Cowynn A Druid of the Sidhe Fuait tribe, under Treon
Daghda A warrior of the Meadhe tribe under Nuada, captured and recruited to Medb's service
Diancecht the Healer A Druid originally of the Meadhe tribe
Domnu A female Fomor, perhaps the strongest of her breed
Ehtne Medb's dressing woman
Ethnui Female Fomor tax collector

Fann Medb's steward
Goibhnui A wandering warrior recruited by Medb
Grainne A beautiful bard, Medb's delegate in Ahascragh
Gwawl A Sligo warrior, Medb's oldest friend, earns the Stone of Might
Indech Brutish Fomor, wears the stolen Stone of Might
Li Ban Medb's scribe, Gwawl's wife
Llud A warrior-ruler, blessed with the Staff of Ferdia
Lleflys A Druid wanderer
Matth Medb's defense advisor
Medb Warrior-queen of the Sligo tribe
Muirne Medb's mother
Nuada the Silver-Handed Ruler of the Meadhe tribe, wields the famous Sword of Nuada
Octriallach Most repulsive of the Fomors, with scars like silver snail-trails
Skatha Warrior-chieftain of Ben Skellig, master sword instructor
Treon Warrior king of the Sidhe Fuait tribe, Medb's treacherous betrothed
Tochmarc Medb's political advisor
Tristan A bard skilled in rune-casting
Ysbaddaden Eire's most power warrior, wields the invincible sword, Answerer

Chapter One

In the last hour of the last day of autumn, light filled the hall of Connaught's citadel to the rafters. It might have been the scene of a celebration, but Queen Medb sat alone beside her blazing fire. Soon she'd have company, more than she wanted, of a nature to darken the brightest chamber.

Every particle of her listened for her fiendish guest, and she jerked when a log popped and threw a spark near her feet. As she stamped out the ember, she brushed her light hair back over her shoulder, then sat motionless again on her stool, staring into the fire with blistering eyes.

Seamaire, her father had called this hall, and sometimes his voice, and those of Medb's mother and brothers, raged so loudly for vengeance from the ravaged stones that it was all she could do not to shout back.

She started violently as the door behind her flung open. But she didn't look around. She didn't want *it* to see how she trembled.

The creature's footsteps crossed toward her. Medb's hands gripped tightly in her lap as an unmistakable stench reached her nose and turned her supper to stone in her belly.

"Whither go your thoughts, tribeswoman?"

That the creature's voice was feminine didn't reassure Medb. She had seen what a female Fomor on a rampage could do. "What do they call you?" she asked.

"I am Ethnui." The thing cackled.

Medb shivered in revulsion. If only she had her sword, or better, Answerer, the invincible sword she'd left behind in Ben Skellig . . .

Tamping down that foolhardy desire, she looked up, daring a quick glance. Ethnui seemed less ugly than some of her Fomor kind. She surely had human blood in her maternal ancestry. Most of the Evil Eye's champions did, though they didn't credit it for the improvement in their looks and intelligence over the common Fomor brute. They simply kept stealing human women. Medb herself had been carried off by a Fomor once, and might well have mothered a half-breed monstrosity like this–if it hadn't been for Ysbaddaden.

Ethnui had the greenish-gray skin of her species, and startling, predatory eyes. A blue fillet held her dark, loose hair, and she wore a necklace of–teeth! Human baby teeth!

Medb quickly looked back at the fire. She shivered again, feeling the creature's grin and gleeful stare.

"It is time for you to pay your taxes," said the fiend.

Medb took a deep breath. And held her tongue.

"You don't object. That's good."

"I have no choice, do I? I'd rather pay than see

the long end of your spear." How she hated this false meekness. The craving to strike this creature boiled within her and her hands itched for the hilt of a sword, any sword.

"Wise, choice, my Lady. Lord Balor requires one-fourth of your grain harvest this year and forty-six of your cattle. Oh, and we'll have ten weight of your metal ore, as well."

"You leave us with very little to last out the winter."

"You'll survive. Cockroaches and humans always survive."

Medb closed her eyes. "Take your tax then, and leave me in peace."

She heard no answer, and feeling a frisson of fear, opened her eyes quickly, only to see that the Fomor had gone, silently, mysteriously, leaving the door wide open to the night's chill mist.

It was over. For another year Medb had held herself in check. Yet she felt as if a vast, silent, white explosion had bloomed inside her head, leaving it vacant.

She forced herself to rise, got up bone by bone, as if she were very old and not still a young woman of only twenty winters. She approached the foggy emptiness beyond the open door. Except it wasn't empty. Blurred balls of torchlight moved by the granaries, the wood piles, the pastures. The Fomors under Ethnui didn't bother to be quiet. Their brutish voices grunted and squealed as they collected the Evil Eye's "taxes." Medb was glad to see no lights in the lodges of her folk. They were all awake, no doubt, but they were wise enough to let the demons take what they wanted without protest. Those with babies would be especially cautious. Fomors delighted in a meal of fresh suckling infant.

Queen Medb clutched herself. It was on a night just like this that the Evil Eye first broke through from the Otherworld. He'd come on horseback, his dark forces bearing torches as they rumbled into Connaught, toward Seamaire, toward the burgh, the fields, the byres. She remembered the wails of her folk, the screams begging, "In the Goddess's name, stop, stop!"

Medb closed the door on those memories as silently as the Fomor fiend had slipped through it, and went back to the fire. "This is the best way," she muttered to the flames.

Many of her people disagreed. Some even thought her a coward, though none would say so to her face. It wasn't cowardice, though, that made her give in to these annual "taxes." Why couldn't her champions and councilors see that it was for them that she looked meek while the Evil Eye's minions took what they wanted?

The Evil Eye. Balor.

She put her hands against her eyes and began to weep, alone in the upper hall of her ruined citadel, tears compounded of rage, impotence, and years of worry.

"This is no good." Medb straightened her back

and fisted her eyes. Looking around the hall again, she saw herself as she had been that terrible night the young Princess Medb came face to face with Balor of the Evil Eye.

Everyone had been at the great citadel of Seamaire that night, all the notables from the three Sligo provinces ruled by Medb's father Aed, along with a large company of Sidhe Fuait from the lands of her betrothed. Though it was the Eve of Samhain, and not an auspicious time to wed, black-eyed Treon had forced the date. "I'll marry Medb now, before you change your mind again, Aed."

Treon had presented his first offer for Medb when she was only fourteen winters. Her father had refused, saying Treon only wanted an alliance so he could forget the Sligo as he went about making war on their less powerful neighbors. But when Medb reached sixteen, Aed relented and agreed to the alliance. She knew it had something to do with the vague and unsettling rumors at work in Eire. An evil power had broken through from the Otherworld with inordinate strength. Even the deafest child heard queer tales, and men who traded with other provinces came home saying curious things.

Aed's Druid priest prophesied, "There's something coming, a great change." No one would explain what that meant, nor how Medb's marriage to Treon and an alliance with the Sidhe Fuait could make a difference.

The night of her wedding, however, all rumors were forgotten. Candles of all sizes and shapes flickered around the hall, illuminating the arrogant figure of Treon, dressed in rich clothing as he stood with folded arms and raised eyebrows.

"Fate, my friends, is always to be respected," he announced. "It is fate that weds the Sligo and the Sidhe Fuait tonight." He smiled shrewdly at Aed.

Medb hated the very sound of his voice, the quickness of his speech, the tenacity of his opinions. Instinct told her there was treachery hidden in him. Standing as far away as the round hall permitted, she wept behind her veil. Her mother, Muirne, put a sympathetic arm around her, but her father, seeing her through the crowd that separated them, narrowed his eyes in anger.

Treon seemed unaware of her altogether, despite the elaborate pains her mother had taken with her appearance. She was dressed as splendidly as her bridegroom, in a gown of gold and silver cloth that complimented her blues eyes and fair hair. But married against her will! How could her father do that to her? She looked around the hall through her tears. There were many strangers present, Sidhe Fuait champions of the three classes–Druids, bards, and warriors–and even some wandering champions, like that young man there with a longish, weather-beaten face. His uncompromising brown eyes revealed an assurance owned by few men so young. If she must wed a stranger, why not a man whose bearing showed resolution and courage rather than Treon's pure greed?

Gwawl should be here. She searched longingly for the broad-boned, ruddy face of her childhood friend, hoping he'd somehow returned to rescue her. Two months ago, Aed had sent him to study under a swordmaster visiting in Ahascragh–conveniently keeping Medb from making any rash demand of him.

Her father gave the signal for the ceremony to begin. But almost at the same instant a sentry called in through the door, "My Lord! Come look at this!"

Aed went to see, and others followed, until everyone streamed out the door, down into the inner court, then up again, onto the wooden palisades of the outer wall. Even Medb trailed along with her mother out into the bleak, colorless fog.

In the gloom of the night pretty balls of light danced along the horizon. They seemed to move with a murmur as faint as air stirring in treetops. Thinking her prayers had come true, that the goddess Danu was coming to stop this ill-conceived marriage, Medb lifted her veils. With every sense she owned she reached out: *Danu, save me!*

Someone laughed and was hushed. "Listen!"

Aed's Druid priest said fatefully, "It's here."

No one asked what he meant, for almost at once the pretty lights became fog-blurred torches, and the murmur grew into the thunder of many horses galloping at great speed. Aed shouted, "To arms!"

The enemies riding out of that fog wore helmets and armor like human warriors, but they were not human. The mounted champions had hideous gray-green skin, and when they opened their mouths, Medb saw spiked teeth. The foot soldiers running behind were giant beasts wearing nothing but furs, a race apart, bred purely for war, as heavy and inhuman as the huge clubs they carried.

"What's that stench?" someone said.

"Fomors!"

Old women in the village told stories of beasts called Fomors. Yet, even seeing them with her own eyes, Medb couldn't believe they had actually broken through from the Otherworld into this of the Tuatha de Dannan.

What happened next happened quickly. Folk scrambled to escape, while Aed's champions rushed for their weapons. The villainous, pillaging Fomors set roof after roof of the burgh afire. Flames crackled, and the mist took on a hellish red glow. Galloping horses neighed, shrieked. Grunting and snarling in their battle fury, the Fomors tossed torches at the foot of Seamaire's outer walls and the logs began to burn.

Aed shouted orders, and Treon did, too, a jumble of commands. "To the forest!" Medb's mother Muirne shouted, pulling Medb down from the burning walls and out the stone arch.

As they started down the sloping mound on which Seamaire was built, a crimson-cloaked monster atop a huge black horse laughed as he rode down Pebre, one of Medb's six brothers. It was Conann, Balor's sword arm on numberless battlefields, known in the legends by a long, gray scar across his deep-set left eye socket. Medb screamed as the brute leaned forward in his saddle wielding a lethal spear called the Gae Bolga. Dozens of barbs in its head ensured Pebre an ugly death. Conann forked him with it and tossed him head over heels. Muirne wailed and ran back up the slope to the mutilated body of her son. Conann wheeled his horse and came back for her.

Medb had no time to register the horror of that next sight, for Conann spied her and started after her. "Mother!" She called out in grief as she ran down the mound blindly, skittering behind a haystack, a stump, a burning lodge. The brute rode after her, his horse's hooves thudding as loudly as Medb's heart. She saw, briefly, her dark-eyed bridegroom mounting a horse, calling his men to follow him. A Fomor champion rode toward them, his oversized battle axe held out. Treon put up a hand and shouted, "Give us leave to retreat and Connaught is yours!"

Medb took this in with one heartbeat, and on the next she heard Conann behind her again. She anticipated the sting of those sharp spear-barbs against her spine–and she felt something she'd never felt in her whole life before: Terror. Terror hit her, a true, primitive gut fear that flooded her veins and ripped at every nerve.

Before Conann could cut her down, the eldest of her brothers, Pater appeared. He thrust her behind him as he faced the monster. Medb had little hope of his success, however, for Pater wielded his sword in such a heavy-footed way. "Danu! Your blessing!" he cried desperately.

Conann toyed with him briefly, then skewered him in one awful swoop. Shaking the youth's body off his spear's barbs with a laugh; he veered toward Medb again.

This time she didn't run. She scooped up her brother's sword and held it ready in both hands. Breathing fast and shallow in that reek of battle smoke, she faced the brute. She had no training, but she would not run again. Leave that for such cowards as Treon.

Conann laughed as he charged his eerie midnight horse right for her, forcing her to duck away from the animal's hooves. As she did, his muscled arm caught her beneath her arms, swung her up, and dropped her across the horse's forequarters.

"Umph!" She lost her grip on her brother's sword. She was helpless, the wind knocked out of her, and knocked out again with each stride of the great horse. Conann laughed at her attempts to right herself. His well-trained horse needed little direction, and he held her down easily with one hand while with the other he went on killing.

At last the mist cleared. The full moon stood high in the sky, illuminating the mayhem. Medb was pulled up. Conann's iron arm squeezed her waist. His breath on her cheek smelled of decay. Swallowing her bile, she tried to judge how best to escape.

Save you strength, she told herself. Don't scream or flail. Wait for your chance.

Many of the Fomors had dismounted and were going about among the slaughtered, hacking off the heads of the noble champions who had tried to resist this assault. The Fomors posted many of these on spears. "A warning to others who would try to stand against us," Conann growled.

Among the mounted heads, Medb's mother's eyes stared at nothing. Medb cried out, forgetting herself and her silence as another Fomor appeared, riding an enormous gray stallion, a dozen hell hounds snapping behind him.

"Lord Balor!" Conann roared in Medb's ear.

She knew that name from the legends, too. As a child she was warned, "Be good, lest you incite Balor's Evil Eye." Seeing him coming through the swirling smoke and fire glare was like seeing an ominous and disquieting phantom. The horns of his bronze helmet stood out eighteen inches on either side of his head, making him taller than he already was. The cold metal blade of his axe dripped blood, and skulls hung from his saddle, knocking together dreadfully. He kept one eye, his evil eye, firmly shut.

The legends said that when he was young, Balor was meddlesome, often intruding on the works of elder Fomors. One day he crept up on a group of spellcasters creating a potion. Ignorant of what magic was at work, he rushed forward to stare into the cauldron. Before the magicians could pull him away, a dash of the potion spat into his eye. Since that time, a mere glance from his stricken socket was a deadly beam. He was forbidden to open it except in battle, and was henceforth called Balor of the Evil Eye.

Medb saw her father now, blood streaming from a wound above his brow. He was held by two Fomor brutes. He shouted, "Conann, before Danu, I order you to let my daughter go!"

Conann laughed. "Your daughter, is she?" He gripped Medb's chin and twisted her head to look at her face. "Fair, she is, too, Aed, and all decked out to be a bride. She'll be *my* bride before this night is done."

"No!" Aed cried.

Conann laughed. "Aye, as you die, King of the Sligo, know that your seed will continue. We have killed all six of your fine sons, but your daughter will live to bear you grandchildren–and they'll be half-Fomor, a great improvement to you line!"

Struggling, Aed turned to Balor. "Lord, mercy for my–"

"Silence!" Balor's voice rolled like thunder and surely could be heard over all of Eire. The demon king didn't speak simply to her father, but to the Tuatha de Dannan:

"Hear me Kings of Eire,
Cowering on your thrones!
Hear me Queens of Eire,
Cowering in your rooms!
Hear me, champions of Eire,
Crying in your drink!

"The mere sound of my name strikes fear into all!
Bone Crusher, Battle Master, Blade Breaker —
Balor of the Evil Eye!

"The isle of Eire is mine now!
There is nothing, no one, who can stop me!
Defiance means death!"

He opened his mouth to laugh, showing his rows of gleaming fangs. Medb would never forget that laugh, so full of slow, heinous triumph.

The monster rode closer to her father. The two Fomor holding Aed stepped aside, leaving the King of the Sligo to stand alone. To his credit, he disdained to look at the beast before him, and instead looked at his daughter.

"Medb, it rests with you."

Those were his last words, for even as Medb opened her mouth to scream, "Run, Father!" Balor leaned forward in his saddle and opened his demonic eye. A painful, searing shaft of light struck Aed, who crumpled under its blast. He slumped to the ground like a suddenly emptied sack. His skin shriveled and darkened, stretching over the bones of his face to uncover a ghastly grin of teeth. His eyes sank into a pair of vacant pits staring sightlessly through scorched, leathery lids. His body withered to an unrecognizable shape with hands shriveled into claws.

When the notorious King of the Fomors shut his evil eye and straightened, he gestured to one of his brutes. "Bring me his head; I want it for my collection."

"No! Father!"

"No, Father!" Conann mocked Medb in a high voice. Reining his black horse around, he laughed, "My Lord Balor preserves the heads of his high-standing victims in cedar oil. He tends them carefully in wooden cases in his hall on Tory Island."

As Balor's lieutenant, Conann rallied the Fomors to go. All Medb's restraint left her as she remembered what he'd threatened earlier: *She'll be my bride before this night is done.* She squirmed and clawed, but he simply grasped her more firmly and finally knocked the side of her head with his spear handle. Then, for a long time, she remembered nothing.

Chapter Two

Medb eventually went to bed that night of the Fomor Ethnui's visit, but she lay awake for long hours remembering how her wedding had turned into a massacre. After what seemed only a few minutes of broken sleep, she was awakened by a hand on her shoulder. Rubbing her weariness from her eyes, she saw that her servant, Ehtne, had stirred the hall's fire back to life and was warming the breakfast gruel.

"Time to rise, my Lady."

Medb sighed, relieved that the night's ugly confrontation was over for another year. She let Ehtne dress her in a woolen skirt and red, round-necked bodice, and after she broke her fast, she went out to share her improved mood with her people.

As she walked down to the burgh, she breathed the salt air. She loved the surge of the breakers that sounded by day and night in Connaught. Though the sea was out of sight behind the forest at the edge of the fields, it was her touchstone, one of the things that even Balor couldn't change.

Her old friend and champion, Gwawl, greeted her as she entered the burgh, and Li Ban gave her a swift, sympathetic hug. "Are you all right?"

Medb gestured her concern away. "It's over, that's all I care about."

"I would have stayed with you, my Lady, willingly." Gwawl's hand rested on the head of the axe in his belt. "Why arm me if I'm not allowed to fight?"

Medb laughed. "Gwawl, you are too fierce for such a happy day. You'll throw fear into the sun itself, and it will hide behind a cloud."

He gave her a reserved look, which she mocked by looking at him cross-eyed, as she had done when they were children together. He relaxed into a ruddy-cheeked grin. "We'll take this up another day then." He put his arm around Li Ban, who was his betrothed.

"Another day," Medb agreed, "when all is snow and ice and we're as grim as the weather."

Despite her giddy relief, Samhain's coming meant that soon the long winter would descend, bringing piercing winds and a cold, low sun. The sea already ran higher, and the bracken in the lowlands had turned red. Nonetheless, today pulsed with light and morning, and Medb meant to stroll through her burgh.

The village boasted several sturdy oval buildings of tightly-chinked logs, all thickly thatched over. Their oaken doors hung on iron hinges burnished with fat until they gleamed. Medb and her companions laughed as they waded through a brace of fat foul fighting over the scraps a villager had thrown out her door.

Medb's easy mood was not shared by her folk, however. The citizens were all whispers and little signals and tight lips today. As she passed a group of three men, one complained, "My best dun milk cow is gone this morning."

"Aye, and my white bull."

"Sweet Danu be merciful, you should see my barn! Not only did the thieves take what they wanted, they scattered grain everywhere–as if we have enough to waste and get through the winter, too!"

Medb felt her smile stiffen. Her people grumbled more about Balor's taxes every year, and today they watched her with disappointment. What did they want? Did they think she could stop the loose demons–she and two warriors?

Finally, pushed forward by his fellows, a townsman blocked her way. "My Lady, may I speak?"

"Your name is Abrat, isn't it?" Medb said. Though he wore an ordinary woolen tunic and leggings, he was unmistakable, for some accident of birth had left his neck permanently hunched forward. "Speak freely," she said, not entirely sure she wanted to hear.

"The folk have asked me to . . . that is . . . " He cleared his throat and craned his bent neck upward to look her in the eye. "There are some who feel we should try to trade again, my Lady. With other tribes. There are things we can't grow here, things we used to get from other provinces . . . " In his nervousness, he twisted his cap in his hands like a *bain sidhe* wringing her bloody laundry.

"What provinces did you have in mind?"

"We thought Elphin. To begin with. The Sidhe Fuait."

Medb looked at the faces in the crowd that had gathered. "Are you sure there *is* an Elphin, or that the Sidhe Fuait tribe still lives there?"

"We've heard . . . things."

So had Medb. Despite her policy of isolation, news from the outside reached Connaught like blown smoke, usually months late, yet inevitably. She'd heard that Treon was still King of the Sidhe Fuait–and still up to his old tricks of looking out for himself first and foremost.

"We thought," Abrat plodded on, "that at least someone could go see. If anyone is in Elphin, that is. Our border is only a river's width from their's. How dangerous could it be?"

A craftsman stepped forward. "We need to see who is left besides us. We can't live all shut up here forever, *my Lady!*"

Gwawl exclaimed at the man's sneering tone, and started forward. Medb caught him with a hand on his arm. When he looked back, she shook her head.

"He shouldn't talk to you that way!"

"It's all right, Gwawl."

She turned her eyes back to the craftsman, who tried to pretend he wasn't shaken by Gwawl's response. He was a noisy fellow, but Medb appreciated the skill that went into his workmanship. Nonetheless, he shouldn't talk to her that way. Controlling her own temper, she said, "And what if there is no one else? What if Fomors occupy the other provinces of Eire?"

"Then we need to find that out, too!" shouted a woman, Guendoloena, once a stout housewife. Now her woolen skirts seemed too heavy for her and her faded yellow-and-blue bodice too loose. She'd been married a year before her husband was killed in the Destruction. She had a child by him, a daughter on whom she doted. The hard times had been doubly hard on them. "I lost a fine fat hog of near three-hundred weight last night. Now my bairn will have to dine on what poor pork we have left from last year." She turned away abruptly, her face in her hands, revealing that her true emotion wasn't anger so much as desperation.

Abrat tried to regain control. "My father used to trade with Donegal to the north, my Lady Queen. If you'd prefer us to try in that direction."

His father had been killed the same night as Medb's own family. All of them had lost loved ones to Balor's slaughter. Her displeasure softened. "It's not the direction, Abrat, it's the danger. I want to protect those of you who are left."

No one seemed to understand that, not even her councilors, who had urged her for a year to send scouts into the neighboring provinces.

Perhaps because she was wrong?

Taking a deep breath, she said, "It shall be as you ask then. I'll send–"

"Me, my Lady!" Her younger champion, Ainle, stepped before her out of nowhere. "Gwawl is to wed shortly, so there is no one else."

Medb looked at him with resignation. "Very well." She raised her voice so that even those in the back of the crowd might hear. "Lord Ainle will go to Donegal, to the north, and we'll see what he finds there."

The people seemed to sigh, as if they'd been holding their breaths. Leaving the burgh, Medb hoped she was doing the right thing. With Ainle gone, she would be short by a third of her defenders.

Since the Assault there were warriors on the roads, brave men of skill left without chieftains to serve. Why shouldn't they join the Sligo and serve her? A few had passed through in the three years of her rule, but none had stayed. How could she lure them? She must take up the matter with her defense advisor, Matth.

She found him with Fann, her steward, taking stock of what the Fomors had left for the winter provisioning of her soldiers. Listening to her question, Matth fingered a medallion he wore. Sliding Fann a glance, he said at length, "We might set up a tent and stock it with good ale and dry beds. Soon enough word will get about that there's welcome to be had with the Sligo."

"I don't want to play hostess to every vagabond on the road. I want to recruit good sword arms. And masters of the natural forces," she added.

Fann tossed her waist-long blond hair over her shoulder. "What better way than to coax these champions and masters into lingering a while, as

Matth suggests? As they take their rest, we can do our foremost to recruit them."

It went against Medb's instinct to welcome, even encourage, strangers across her borders. But perhaps shoring up her defenses was worth the risk. She nodded. "I'll trust you, Fann, to see to it."

"Consider it done, my Lady."

The muscles around Matth's jaw tightened into a rare smile.

Medb started away, but at the door she turned back briefly. "Oh, and Fann, send a barrel of our best pork to poor Guendoloena and her daughter."

It took Ainle two months to return through the snows of Samhain with news of his explorations. "The Goddess has blessed us, my Lady. Donegal holds nothing more than a few scattered, fearful folk who have no leader. Those I spoke to would be glad to come under your rule. Indeed, they're fearful that King Treon will claim them for the Sidhe Fuait. They don't like Treon."

All four tongues of Medb's councilors began to wag at once. Even quiet Matth showed more emotion than Medb had ever seen. "We must send settlers at once. If we don't claim it, Treon surely will."

"There is some risk in claiming this land," she reminded them. "We'll have to send one of our champions, and he'll naturally want to take his family and the folk loyal to him. That means that we will accomplish less here and be susceptible to attack."

"If Treon takes Donegal, it places his power at our very borders," Li Ban said.

"And if he hasn't taken a wife yet, and decides to claim you are still his betrothed . . . " Fann hesitated.

White bearded Tochmarc finished the sentence for her. "It would give him an excuse to claim all your lands."

"Let him try," Medb muttered darkly.

"Nonetheless–"

"We have no choice, I know."

She would send Ainle to settle Donegal with his family, servants, and all those loyal to him. When told the news, his boyish eyes flashed. "I thank you for your trust, my Lady. And for this opportunity for my folk to prosper. Though, of course, I shall miss you."

Medb smiled. He was so young. He saw the years of struggle and work ahead of him as something to look forward to, as much more exciting than drifting in the backwater of Connaught. Medb, on the other hand, wished she could do nothing more than drift here.

During those last months of winter, both humans and animals declined and sickened, since Balor's Fomors had taken so much of their stores. The most generous repast added up to grain porridge and ale, with perhaps a few leaves of stewed winter cabbage or an onion. Yet the air crackled with agitation as the emigrants packed. Ainle planned to leave as soon as the snows melted. He hoped to reclaim a cluster of abandoned farms in Donegal in time to put crops in the ground.

Medb saw them off on a day of heavy rain and wretched mud. She gave Ainle a brief, hard embrace. "You'll not make the best time in this weather, I fear. Yet it might mean a safer passage than if the skies were fine. Whatever comes, Ainle, I shall pray to Danu for your safety."

"We go with good hope, my Lady. We'll establish a province you'll be proud to call Sligo."

"I haven't a doubt of it." She didn't try to hide the tears in her eyes. She felt as if she were losing one of her brothers all over again. "Go with the Goddess, my friend."

When the last of the caravan passed from sight, the folk left behind went about their business with a sort of miserable air. They had lost so many to Balor's assault, and now to lose more . . . the air was thick with sadness.

The arrival of the Feast of Imbolc helped, bringing the long-awaited marriage of Li Ban and Gwawl. Medb was happy for her friends. But she wondered when, or if, she would ever find love.

Spring greened the landscape and encouraged the plowmen and the planters. Bran, Medb's young Druid priest, cast a spell to increase the Connaught's forests, and Medb found new seedlings within the week. She received a message from Ainle, delivered by a slight, nervous native of Donegal who repeated Ainle's words by rote: "Bless the soil I stand on. We have arrived and settled, and are starting to build up the burgh." Grainne, Medb's representative in Ahascragh, also sent a report to her queen. Her herds had been blessed with thirty calves, and she planned to begin a mining operation soon. From Clifden, the Druid Caipre sent word that affairs were moving smoothly.

The tent set up to attract free-roaming Druids, bards, and swordsmen had stood empty throughout snowy Samhain, but now solitary guests began to accept the open-handed hospitality of the Sligo tribe. Medb heard tidings that were mostly forbidding, of a lingering darkness from the Otherworld that seemed to favor an increase in wars between men. Tribal loyalties were betrayed and oaths forgotten. It was all a part of the Evil Eye's destructive design.

With each new visitor, Medb learned a little more about the state of Eire outside her borders. Her main purpose remained, however, to recruit more warriors for herself. This became imperative when she received a strained message from Ainle that his herds had been raided by members of Treon's tribe.

"Lord Ainle fears that King Treon sent the raiders to scout Donegal's defenses–which are not strong, my Lady Queen." The slight, nervous man at least spoke with his own words this time. "We fear that Treon will come exactly as the Evil Eye did, to loot and leave the land in ruin."

Medb felt her old anger well up again, but what to do about it? Sending Gwawl or going herself would put Connaught in the same position of having only one champion on the defense.

As she fretted over this, Fann came to her, brushing her long shining hair out of her eyes and saying, "Happy news! Not one, but two champion warriors have chosen to rest from their wanderings in our tent."

Within the hour, Medb and Gwawl had ridden out to the tent, located north of the citadel. "Hail and high greetings, my Lords!" Gwawl called.

The flap lifted, and Medb encountered a man she'd heard much about, even before the Destruction. Arawn was a renowned warrior. His collar-length hair, combed straight back, was a dark red, and his mustache and goatee were an even darker shade. Bowing, he said in a rumbling voice, "My Lady Queen. I once met your father." He seemed unhappy to see a mere woman in charge of the Sligo now, however.

"My father is gone, and all my brothers."

He nodded sharply, only a little less remote than the moon. "Accept my sympathy."

He didn't ask about her mother, another useless woman, Medb supposed.

The second guest came to his feet as she entered the tent. He wore a wide cloth headband to hold back his long blond hair. His thick mustache was blond, too.

"Fair Lady, may I introduce Goibhnui, looking for danger and adventure like myself," said Arawn.

But Goibhnui wasn't at all like Arawn. His good looks masked a fox-like cunning that Medb mistrusted.

"Please, be at ease, my Lords. We have brought you a new-baked loaf and a wheel of cheese."

Gwawl placed the food basket on the tent's small table, and added a flagon and four cups. "There's a drop of wine here, too, made from the grapes of my own vines. I think you'll find it sweet and quenching."

Medb seated herself at the table, and the three men followed her lead. The tent held two beds, the table with its stools, and the visitors' packs, weaponry, and battle armor.

Goibhnui took charge of Gwawl's flagon, and poured them all wine. Arawn pulled his belt knife to cut the cheese.

"You look weary, my Lord," Medb said.

"I have traveled far, but conversation always lifts my spirits," Arawn rumbled casually.

"I've heard much of your skill. Your reputation travels before you."

"I know a little of swordcraft."

"But then, so do you, my Lady," said Goibhnui suddenly. "At least, so says the reputation that travels before *you*. Though I must admit, you're not what I expected. You don't even wear a sword."

Gwawl looked puzzled, and Medb felt herself flush. "That was a long time ago."

"What was?" Arawn asked.

"Have you news of the world beyond my borders?" she asked.

"There is little out there to compare to the dream that was Eire before it was destroyed by Balor."

She shivered to hear that name said aloud. "Are there many tribes still intact?"

"In some form or other, yes. The winds bring word that the Tir Tairn especially have grown powerful."

"Indeed." Medb's father had always said the ruler of the Tir Tairn was a man to watch out for.

"What about the Sidhe Fuait?" Gwawl asked.

Arawn shrugged. "Treon is looking to build his power, as always."

Medb nodded. "We may have a problem with Treon. One of my champions recently emigrated to Donegal, where the folk were left scattered. He reports that Treon seems interested in Donegal as well."

Arawn busied himself with the cheese again.

"Our problem is in our lack of numbers. I most desperately . . . " She shouldn't use that word. "It's *important* for me to send him help. But there are only Gwawl and me here in Connaught. My other provinces are being looked after by a talented bard and a Druid priest, very capable, but neither of them warriors. Meanwhile, my folk in Donegal live in unfortified villages . . . " She stopped at Arawn's blank look of boredom.

"We need warriors." She couldn't be more concise than that.

Goibhnui seemed amused. “I believe my Lady is trying to recruit you, Arawn.”

“And you,” Medb said quickly. “I could use you as well.” She might not like his manner, but he owned a sword.

A slight feral grin, “I wonder how badly you want us, my Lady.” He glanced at Arawn. “Did you know that Lady Medb was a student of Skatha? She actually trained with Ysbaddaden–and did well, by all accounts.”

Arawn studied her with new interest, while Gwawl turned a stupefied look her way. “What's this?”

“As I said, that was a long time ago. I've let my skills lapse.”

“What skills?” Gwawl asked, at the same time that Arawn said, “A great mistake, my Lady.”

Goibhnui, eyes dancing, said, “I'm sure you'd finish me off in a moment, for I never trained with so great a teacher as Skatha, but I wonder how you'd do against someone as acclaimed as my Lord Arawn.”

“Is that where you were?” Gwawl asked. “In Ben Skellig, with this Ysbaddaden?”

She met his eyes. “Skatha gave us both training, yes, though of course Ysbaddaden ever had the better arm. Better than anyone's, I'd warrant.” She slid Arawn a glance.

He said thoughtfully, “I'd like to put that to the test. Oh aye, I would.”

Ignoring the questions in Gwawl's eyes, Medb glanced at Goibhnui with distaste, then at Arawn. She needed him; Ainle needed him. She would not lose loved ones again to Treon's selfishness.

"I have tested myself against Ysbaddaden many a time," she said, "and since he is unavailable, perhaps you would consent to try me in his place? I assure you, he taught me almost as much as Skatha did."

The warrior's eyelids lowered a fraction. "I had no idea when I came–"

"No," she cut in. "After all, I'm only a woman."

Her resentment amused him. "And I have the manners of a rotten Fomor. Forgive me, my Lady Queen, for underestimating you. It would be an honor if you would spar with me."

She inclined her head. "What I have in mind is not just a simple sparring match. I have my terms."

"And what would those be?"

"Since I don't claim Ysbaddaden's strength, nor Skatha's skill, you will win. We both know it already." Her heart thudded with her audacity. "But, if I can draw the great Arawn's blood before he can draw mine, will you give me your oath of allegiance and help my champion keep Donegal from Treon?"

"Your price is high."

"Your sword is sharp. Sharper by far than mine. And your arm longer. And your experience greater. It would seem you have little to lose."

No one so much as breathed while the swordsman turned the matter over in his mind. Finally, he pushed his empty cup toward Goibhnui for refilling. "I like your mettle, my Lady Medb. We'll meet on your practice field tomorrow morning."

Tomorrow! The air around Medb seemed to toll with a silent percussion. She'd hoped for a few days to brush up on her skills, "Tomorrow it is, then." She lifted her cup and drank. As she swallowed, she awarded Goibhnui an icy smile. "Of course, you'll meet me under the same terms the day after the morrow?"

His eyes winked like a fox's. "I'd be honored, my Lady Queen. I've lived through a number of battles, but I still strive to hone the skills Danu gave me–and how better?"

He too drank, then said, "Have you seen Ysbaddaden lately?"

Her heart skipped. "Not lately, no."

"I saw him in Sneem a year ago. He'd come from Kilcullen, fought over for years now by every chieftain along her unending borders. I forget which side Ysbaddaden fought for, but when the chieftain accepted an offering of gold to retreat, Ysbaddaden left his service. He's looking for a leader to unite Eire, you know. He's a dreamer." Goibhnui shrugged. "But a man to be feared, nonetheless."

Medb wanted to ask a thousand questions: How does he fare? Is he healthy? Before she could make a fool of herself in that manner, Arawn said, "Last I heard of you, you were to wed Treon."

Medb straightened her thoughts. "Our betrothal

was nullified by the Evil One's raid on Connaught–and by the bargain he made with Conann to withdraw, thereby allowing the Fomor fiends to butcher us."

She rose to go. All three men stood, and Goibhnui swept her a low bow. In return, she gave him a look that could have shaved him. Her blade was bound to lose against Arawn, but her temper would score this fox's smooth trickery.

Gwawl followed her out into the blue evening. As they mounted their horses, she knew he roiled with questions that she wasn't up to answering just now. She said, "I'd like to be alone a while. Will you ride back and tell Ehtne I'll be late for my supper?"

"Medb . . . " It wasn't often he addressed her as he had during the easy friendship of their youth.

"I know you don't understand, Gwawl. One day I'll tell you everything, but not now . . . please?"

Though troubled, he nodded. "I'll speak to Ehtne."

As he rode off at a sharp canter, she watched him with regret. She didn't really want to be alone, but since his marriage, being with him was often the same as being alone.

She brought her thoughts up short. Was she jealous? Certainly she wished both her friends all their joy. But sometimes it seemed so harsh that she'd had her chance and forfeited it. And for what? More and more it seemed that Ysbaddaden may have been right all along.

Talking and thinking of him was like ripping a crusted bandage off a festering wound. Perhaps she did need some time alone.

She took a path that led her through the forest to a secluded place by the sea, about a half-hour's ride from her fortress. She left her horse and climbed to a spot familiar only to her. Though there was no trail, her feet knew the way out of habit. She came out on an open headland and stood on the very edge of the day. Gazing out at the open sea, it seemed she heard the restless whinnies of horses and the sound of inhuman singing–the memories were that close. She looked down at the tide thundering at the base of the cliff. The Druids said all life began in the sea. Her own life had begun its second half underwater, in a place much like that below.

Chapter Three

The night Conann had carried Medb away from Seamaire, intending to make her his unwilling bride, she lay in a dark, foreboding dream when she heard herself called, as from a great distance. For a while, she continued to float in the dark, doing nothing, anticipating nothing, fearing nothing.

"Princess!"

As consciousness returned, instinctively her mind recoiled.

"Princess Medb! If you don't wake up, they're going to take you to Tory Island!"

It was no good. Her mind would awaken. She felt fingertips petting her cheek as the voice went on urgently: "Princess!"

Her head hurt, her tongue tasted foul, she felt drugged. She awoke fully–to terror, because she heard *them* singing. The Tuatha de Dannan were a song-loving people, the Fomors sang to a music like nothing she'd ever heard.

"Aye, that's it," said the whisper, "keep your eyes open now. Don't move, just be quiet. They're carousing behind you, but they're not watching you, not closely anyway."

She could hardly make sense of the words, but he kept on until she realized where she was. The fingertips on her cheek and the voice belonged to a man lying as flat to the ground as he could, mostly hidden by shadow and bracken. Only his hand reached out to wake her. She couldn't see his face, just the reflection in his eyes of the huge Fomor fire blazing behind her.

He said she shouldn't move. So she let her senses guide her. Her left arm was bent beneath her and had no feeling in it. She'd been tossed with no care from Conann's saddle at the edge of the fiends' camp. Like a wounded animal. Like prey.

At least she was downwind of them. Sounds were carrying from them to her, not from her to them. But so was their stench.

"Listen to me. No one is looking just now, but he could remember you any time."

Terror seized her.

"What I want you to do is creep this way–slowly! Don't attract attention."

Medb tried to do as he said, because stranger or not, he was her only hope. She eased her left arm out from under her, but it was so bloodless she could only pull it along at first as she inched slowly into the bracken, following as he backed away in the same manner. Propelled by her toes and knees and elbows, breathing the cold earth and leaf mold, she followed his lead.

Her arm tingled maddeningly when he allowed her to sit up. "Who are you?"

He'd half-risen to see if the way was clear to

make a run for it. He dropped back down. "My name is Ysbaddaden. I was at your wedding; I saw them take you."

"And you followed them?" She rubbed her arm to bring back the blood, not quite sure why anyone would be so foolish. "Why?"

"Shh." He helped her up. "Keep low."

She rose to his level, but her head swam, and he let her lean with it resting against his shoulder. He led her toward the sea.

Before they reached it, they heard shouts and bawled orders. Balor's hell hounds began to bay. "He's discovered you're missing." Ysbaddaden hurried her to a cliff, impossibly steep and offering no footholds. She stared at the uproar and confusion of the out-sweeping tide below. They were trapped. Conann would get her. Death was preferable. Better to leap and die. Summoning all her strength, she looked down into the roar of angry water below.

Ysbaddaden's hand in the small of her back suddenly pushed. She lost her footing, gasped, flailed–and fell! She cursed Ysbaddaden–if she had to jump, she'd rather do so of her own volition! She screamed as her body turned a half-somersault, and then she struck the water, on her back.

Underwater. Cold. Dazed. Disoriented. She couldn't tell which way was up. A surge of current tumbled, and she bobbed to the surface. She came up choking, lashing out with her hands but clutching only air.

Something big splashed beside her. A swell rose beneath her, bearing her high on its crest. She couldn't see anything but great undulating swells of blue-black ocean. The tide was taking her out. She was going to die. She screamed again–the scream of a vital being protesting death. Panicked, she forgot how to swim. She thrashed about, then felt an arm around her waist. A voice said, "I've got you! It's all right!" Ysbaddaden. Her hands grabbed whatever they could find of him. He pulled her against him and against the out-sweeping tide, saying, "It's all right! Help me!"

They reached for handholds on the rocks at the base of the cliff. Ysbaddaden hauled her up with him onto a submerged shelf. Only their heads and arms were above the water, and not even their heads when the next wave broke against the cliff. Surging out again, the wave tried to take them with it. Medb felt her legs sucked away from the shelf. Ysbaddaden reached for her, missing her hand by inches. But a new swell raised her up, and dropped her down again, and this time his hand caught her fingertips and pulled against the suck of the tide. He pulled so hard she thought her fingers might come out of their joints. Then her hand again touched the hard cliff rocks. Coughing and gasping, she struggled to hold on to the very edge of her homeland.

Their hiding place was completely exposed to the sea, but in the dark, could those searching for them above see them? She prayed that they couldn't. She heard a hound yelping directly above them. "Get back!" came a voice. As if kicked, the animal yelped away. Balor's unmistakable voice shouted, "She was mad, Conann! She leapt to her death! Leave her to the sharks!"

The two waited in the water another hour, however, before they began the precarious climb to safety in the gathering light. They gained the top of the cliff and stood in the sunrise tentatively, with their arms crossed over their chests, hands tucked into armpits, shivering. Were the Fomor really gone?

It would seem so. And Medb was safe from Conann. Ysbaddaden reclaimed his traveler's pack and armor and sword left high up in the crotch of a tree. And when he started out, she let him lead her where he would.

For days she followed him through endless forests of huge trees, through marshes, through bracken, and over stony outcrops. She followed, disoriented, beyond tears, numbed by a sense of aloneness. She had no parents, no brothers–she'd never conceived of being so alone before. It left her feeling cold and naked.

They ate whatever they found, the round loaf left on the table of a deserted lodge, a stray goose honking noisily in a marsh, honey from a scorched bee tree. They caught fish in deep pools with their fingers and ate them raw. A princess raised on delicacies such as rabbit fetuses poached in milk, Medb now ate whatever was put into her mouth.

When the first snow fell, they took refuge in a cave where Ysbaddaden shared his cloak with her.

As soon as the weather cleared, they fashioned rude snowshoes and Medb went on, slowly and clumsily, beyond pain, beyond exhaustion, beyond anything.

More days passed, and still Ysbaddaden led her away from all she knew. When she faltered, he caught her arm; when she fell, he hauled her up. He never seemed to tire the way she did.

They were going south, moving along the old Celtic trackways that wound about the rock-edged coast. When Ysbaddaden turned east and started inland, Medb wondered if he had a destination in mind or if he were simply running. If escape was his aim, it was useless, for everywhere they saw the same smoking ruins, the same razed crops, the same empty pastures. Balor's minions had leveled all of Eire. Everything the monster had said seemed true; the island was his now, and there was no one, nothing, to stand against him.

Ysbaddaden took the precaution of skirting any community they happened upon. "Whoever is left could turn vicious, bent on protecting whatever they have. Best not to ask for help."

Bruised, lacerated, frostbitten, Medb didn't agree or disagree. A part of her understood that he was talking about the panic Balor had sown with his savagery, but the rest of her had gone as numb as her arm that first terrible night.

They even avoided other groups journeying like themselves–or not like themselves, for those others were looking for lost kindred and neither she nor Ysbaddaden had kindred now.

Without being aware of actually hearing him tell it, she'd absorbed his history. He'd been wandering from place to place when he'd chanced upon her wedding party in Seamaire. He'd lost his family to a Fomor raid months earlier. The uncle who had reared him was killed, and his two little cousins carried off to be Fomor slaves. "I didn't know how much they mattered to me until they were gone." Revenge was the one thing he craved, to help expiate his sin of being absent at the time of the raid on his family.

At last, one late afternoon, he said, "We're here."

Medb climbed to stand beside him at the top of a knoll that formed the only bridge into a stony, hilly peninsula province. Her eyes saw; her spirit was elsewhere. Clouds streamed eastward. Beneath them, in the lowering darkness, lay yet another burned-out village. A few folk were doing their last chores–what work there was left to do. Uninterested, she touched a blood-crusted briar cut on her cheek, and scratched at her matted hair. She knew only two things: her weariness and the pain gnawing at her empty stomach.

"This is Ben Skellig, Skatha's province," Ysbaddaden said. "There's her citadel."

Medb saw the stone tower atop a stony promontory.

Unlike Seamaire, its palisades had not been reduced to ashes, for they were built of the same stone that lay everywhere except in the cleared fields. It still had its full three stories, too, and a roof.

She'd heard of Skatha, of course. But why had Ysbaddaden brought her here?

He was looking at her. He didn't say anything more, just bent down and kissed her forehead. Her eyes saw him: a face, under its dirt and thick beard, still young and very handsome, but already marked with suffering and disappointment. He had seemed so much older, so suspicious and controlled, until now. Why had he kissed her? She didn't care enough to ask, only fell into step behind him once more as he led her down into the village.

She couldn't recall their reception, or even if she'd met Skatha. The next thing her memory recalled was a dream of home and dawn and breakfast. She smelled porridge and tried to weave it into her dream, but instead her eyes opened. She saw light spilling over her, and heard an unusual but definitely female voice say, "Good morning, drowsy eyes."

She raised her head groggily to see a strong woman standing over her. The dazzle of light came through a window. The woman's face glimmered in it.

She sat on the edge of Medb's bed box–yes, she was in a real bed, and furthermore, she was clean, her hair was clean, her hands, she wore a clean undergown. The woman offered a cup of broth.

"Drink up."

That voice–it was crisp and rich, Medb decided, like the first bite of a tart apple. "Thank you," she said automatically, squinting in that diamond-bright sunshine. She felt as if she'd wakened inside a bright jewel.

"Goddess be, you're blinking like a mole. I shouldn't wonder. After two days of sleep I suppose you can hardly take in the real world again."

Two days? She looked back through the unaccountable lost hours, and vaguely recalled wading through dream after murky dream, some of them savage and primal, some wishful and yearning.

"Are you Lady Skatha?"

Her hostess bowed her glinting, sun-anointed head. "I am. And you are Lady Medb, Queen of the Sligo."

Queen of the Sligo? Her mind resisted the title, but then admitted it must be true, with all her family but her dead.

"Ysbaddaden tells me you have it in you to become a great warrior."

A warrior? "Where would he get that idea?" Medb stared at her in amazement.

Skatha laughed again. Her eyes were warm, and her nose had a scattering of freckles. And she was dressed beautifully. Evidently the Fomor had not found her clothing chest. "He says you picked up a sword, ready to challenge Conann himself."

Medb lowered her eyes. The mere mention of

Conann's name brought back the foul-smelling nearness of him. "If I did, I acted without thought. I know nothing of swordcraft."

"Tell your young warrior that. He wanted to wake you yesterday. Wouldn't rest himself. He's very eager to begin."

"Begin what?"

"You don't know? He wants me to teach him what I can of sword skill. And you, if you care to learn a few things."

"But I'm only a girl."

The pleasant face sobered somewhat. "You are the hope of your people, Medb."

Cold fingers brushed her spine. *Medb, it rests with you,* her father had said just before Balor seared him with his evil eye.

"If nothing else, you should know how to defend yourself should a Fomor ever decide to steal you again."

"Yes, I would like to be able to defend myself."

"Very well then. We'll begin as soon as you're fed and dressed." She stood. The freckled face smiled down. "Ysbaddaden will be glad to hear you're awake. He's been wringing his hands over you."

Medb frowned at the image of the unrelenting youth who had forced her on and on over the weeks past. "Is he well? I assume so. He's so . . . sturdy."

"Sturdy? Aye, he is that. And resolute. He wouldn't begin his own instruction without you. This should be interesting," she added. "Join us when you can." Still smiling, she went out leaving Medb to her porridge.

Medb came back to herself, brushing away the sands that counted those hours and days long past. As she turned from the seascape and started back, slowly, for her citadel, her mind swiftly took up it's routine responsibilities. She would need to see into her father's old mines, as Graine was doing in Ahascragh. Now was the time to accumulate next winter's firewood. And she should clear some new land for farming.

Thus her mind returned safely from the brink of those memories of Ysbaddaden . . . and Ceridwen's prophecy . . . which were so dangerous and seductive.

She wasn't successful, however, for she woke in the night worrying. In that dark hour, she felt suddenly aware of the humankind all around her, downstairs in the garrison, in the burgh, in the outlying farm lodges. All those lives unknowing of their prospects and depending on her.

She looked back on that time in Ben Skellig again, and she saw it as if it were a lighted window glowing in the distance. Ceridwen must have seen it so. The Druid priestess arrived at Skatha's citadel the very morning Medb woke from her two days of sleep. When Medb came into the hall, she saw Skatha, Ysbaddaden, and the priestess seated at the long table. She gave Ysbaddaden a timid smile; his eyes crinkled as he rose and gestured to the bench beside him. He seemed suddenly very tall and russet-haired and tan.

Skatha immediately introduced Ceridwen as a powerful priestess of the Mysteries and furthermore, a great seeress. "She can see what was and what is going to be."

Ceridwen clasped her hands together before her face, then toward Medb in the traditional greeting of a Druid. For a priestess, she was young. She had a longish face, with very blue eyes, and dark hair. Medb thought she was pretty, though it seemed impious to consider a Druid that way.

"You have traveled the length of Eire," the priestess said to her.

Medb nodded, ill at ease under that intense stare. She let her eyes lower to the Druid's white, graceful hands, folded together on the table. She had long spidery fingers.

"Then you have seen the hunger and plague that stalk the countryside. The folk have turned, illogically, from allies to adversaries. For that we can be grateful to the savage Evil Eye. And it won't end there. We shall suffer again and again unexpected attacks by the Fomors, and a constant thieving of our resources."

Medb didn't know if an answer was required, so she kept quiet. She was aware of Skatha's bright eyes watching for her reaction. What should it be?

"You have great dangers ahead of you, my Lady Queen. They will change you."

Queen. The title nettled her. She gave the Druid a pleading look, and realized that there had been no alteration in the woman's masked face since she'd begun talking to her. Was she in a trance?

"To destroy Balor is the only way to save the tribes. There will arise a ruler who will unite the Tuatha de Dannan and bring down our foe. This is your obligation, Medb."

Medb blinked. "*I* am to discover this king, this ruler?" How was she to do that?

Then, all at once, she was afraid. Her heart stuttered and froze. Ice poured down her back. Ceridwen's eyes caught her and held her, as motionless as a field mouse under the shadow of a great hawk.

"You *are* her, Medb. You will be that great queen."

The fire crackled, but otherwise silence filled the room. Medb dragged in a long breath. "Why are you saying this?" She looked from Ceridwen into Skatha's solemn face, then to Ysbaddaden, and back to Ceridwen as rage broke through her numbness. "No!" She wanted to fight, wanted to rant and defy and storm around. But she swallowed it.

She felt something in her head, like a fish shimmering past, a silken flutter. Ceridwen had touched her mind. Everything she couldn't express in that moment was known to the priestess. Ceridwen looked on her with compassion, but didn't demand less from her. She reached down and brought up a long sheathed object, placing it on the table.

"Danu has sent this to you."

Medb stared at the shape but didn't touch it. At last, Skatha said, "May I?"

Ceridwen inclined her head.

Skatha unwrapped the object, a beautiful sword, crafted with a brilliant blue stone in its hilt.

"It is called Answerer," Ceridwen said, "and it is all but invincible."

No one else said anything for a long moment, until practical Skatha spoke as if to herself. "You shall need proper training to use it, of course."

Ceridwen still held Medb's gaze; Medb was aware of Ysbaddaden, too, frowning as he looked at the enchanted sword.

Skatha continued in her sensible manner. "You will live with me for the time being, and we will learn what talents for sword work you may own. I think you'll cause me seven kinds of misery–but you just may be worth it."

Ysbaddaden was a better swordsman than Medb from the beginning. Yet she learned that she had more skill than she'd ever guessed. When she was a young girl, she'd often bested her brothers. But as they grew older, they refused to spar with her anymore. She assumed it was because she was a mere girl. Now she wasn't so sure they weren't afraid,

afraid that she would show them up.

There was no chance of showing Ysbaddaden up, however. She stood again on the sparring ground, facing him as Skatha watched. The sinews of Ysbaddaden's neck showed like cables, his arms and thighs bulged with strength, and his sweat-sheened face compressed with concentration as her blade flew at him. He fought back coolly and calmly. "You fight like a woman! Like a witch. Yield!"

She wouldn't.

"Careful, Princess!"

He continued to call her Princess even though, as Skatha and Ceridwen had both pointed out, Medb was now a queen. Hard pulse-beats drummed in her head. She was winded, which irritated her. She envied him–the ease of his body, as powerful as an animal's. She wished she were as strong and fast. How did it feel to be so dangerous, to have shoulders as wide as a door? Skatha insisted it was intelligence and skill that won sword battles, but as Medb flexed her fingers to quell the cramps in them, and shifted her weight to ease the strain on her arms and shoulders, she knew that strength certainly helped.

"Careful!" Ysbaddaden came in low with his blade. She swept her sword to meet it an instant too late. The unsharpened edge of his bronze practice sword cut into the bony side of her knee. Even through the protective leather pad she wore, the blow was painful.

"Do you yield?" he asked, dancing back to reset his stance, holding his sword ready for her next attack. At least he was huffing.

But the pain in her knee was serious. It took all her will not to throw her sword aside and clutch herself with both hands. He always won. She felt sick with the humiliation of it. She should do as he said, yield. She had no alternative. And if she didn't, he would call her names some more, and laugh at her, and sooner or later wound her again.

Skatha, standing off the field, shouted instructions that were shredded by the wind. Medb couldn't hear them, and it would be ruinous to look away from Ysbaddaden now.

"You're too used to sparring with dairymaids. I'll never yield."

His eyes, brown and level, registered the meaning of her insult, and he smiled almost indulgently as he stalked leisurely forward. As happened sometimes, a change came over him. He was moving in for the kill. She felt fear, but she feared his contempt more. That was why she never yielded.

But Skatha stepped onto their fighting ground before he could bring the match to a conclusion, a signal that they should both lower their blades. "Medb, I can't believe you didn't catch that sweep. You'll lose your leg to a sharp blade one day if you aren't ready for that move." Her quiet voice judged the matter coolly, as if it were an everyday thing to lose one's leg. With her own sword in her hands–a fully sharpened sword–Skatha faced Ysbaddaden herself, nodding at him to try his low sweep against her.

Skatha was a vigilant teacher, who favored showing over telling, doing over talking. Not only did she catch Ysbaddaden's thrust, but her parry twisted his blade in a way that caused his arm to fly out wildly. "There! And now I continue in–" The point of her blade stopped a scant inch from his leather-protected belly. "See?"

Skatha pulled her weapon back. "And he's just been sent to his rest with the Goddess Mother. You see, Medb?" She demonstrated the twisting technique more slowly. "Learn it, then don't think about it again. Just do it."

Now that she knew Skatha better, Medb realized there were many things the swordswoman didn't think about, usually the very things she was best at. It was a skill Medb found difficult, turning off her mind, acting with her thoughts dead still.

"You have it," Skatha said, as Medb practiced the twist. Medb nodded.

"Then show *me,*" Ysbaddaden said in a low voice as he came at her with an impudent cock of his eyebrow.

On they sparred. Her arms and shoulders shrieked before the day's exercise ended when a herdsman reported to Skatha the onset of a sudden disease among the cattle. "Fomors brought it in the night," he said, frightened. "I saw them, my Lady."

Skatha nodded grimly. "One of them visited me, too."

Medb shuddered. "They were here? Last night?"

"Delivering threats and warnings, yes."

And she hadn't said anything before now? Medb wondered how she could be so cool. She wanted to ask, but Skatha deflected all serious conversations before they plumbed too deeply.

"I will go see what can be done for the herd. We absolutely need the few head of cattle we have left."

As Skatha left, Ysbaddaden stood spraddle-legged, hands on his thighs as he stared at the packed earth beneath the grass of their practice yard, catching his breath. Medb walked around in small circles as her own breath caught up with her heart. Straightening, he smiled a certain slow smile he had, and threw his arm easily over her shoulders, sheltering her like a canary under the wing of an eagle. With his sword arm, he made a wordless sweeping gesture at the horizon. Medb nodded that she appreciated the wonderful day, too.

"Let's walk."

They left their swords with a servant and headed for the seashore which lay beyond the greening fields. Climbing to the top of a knoll in a weary zigzagging way, they trotted down the opposite side to the sandy beach. A few men worked at a distance mending nets.

"You know, Princess, I've been giving it thought, and there has to be a great battle."

Medb felt the usual creeping unease as he brought up this subject again. Ceridwen had gone, but her impossible and unfair prophecy remained like a yoke around her neck.

"A great battle in which order will take over from these primitive beings and bring harmony back to the land."

Medb pushed herself away from the lofty words, and from their speaker.

"A lot of little battles, to gather us all together under one ruler," he went on, unnoticing, "then a great battle to reclaim our souls."

He stretched his long arms over his head, until his back cracked, then stooped to pick up a stone and toss it into the tumbling surf. Medb felt something loosen inside her. He was such a handsome young man, a man to look at more than once. He was twenty-four winters old, strongly made, with thick, red-brown hair, and a coloring burned by the sun to a shade rarely seen except in autumn leaves and aged ale. His body was pure power, even in repose. As she stared, he turned, and looked deeply into her eyes.

"Once the High Ruler is named, Balor will have to surface and confront the leader over the lordship of Eire." His touch on her arm felt sunny and light. "And you're the one. Do you think the Goddess sent me to rescue you? I do. One day you'll be the High Ruler of Eire, Princess. You'll wear the Lia Fail, the Stone of Destiny, and then you'll defeat Conann and Balor."

No! She'd never have the strength or experience to do all that! Nor the courage. Perhaps Skatha could do it, perhaps even Ysbaddaden himself, but her? Never! She backed away from him. "Why do you shrink from it?"

"You've seen what the Evil Eye can do. If anyone were to try this scheme of yours, and she failed–can't you imagine the horror that would follow?"

His expression told her that he couldn't foresee failure at all, and that what he'd witnessed of Balor's destruction had left him angry, but unafraid.

She turned, desperate to hide her own fear from him. She started to run along the edge of the foamy surf. "Let's wake up the waterbirds!"

They ran together into the nesting grounds, and soon were laughing in a cloud of wings as the indignant birds rose up around them.

When she flung herself down on a sandy slope of long, dry grass, and lay on her back, breathing hard again, he lowered himself beside her, and lay on his side, his head propped on his elbow. "You have a nice laugh."

She didn't answer, only looked up at the long strips of white cloud scudding across the brilliant sky. They had never been anything but casual with one another, but in her private, unspoken yearnings, Medb knew she wanted more. His callused palm, dry and warm, moved on her cheek. But when she saw his expression, saw him swallow, saw his head start to lower toward hers, she rolled away and sat up.

"Well parried." He fell onto his back.

She shivered, as she sometimes did, as though some large presence had moved at the edge of her vision. She snapped her head to the right, then to the left. Nothing.

Blowing out a hard breath, she busied herself with taking off the various leather pads that protected her legs and arms during their practice sessions. She had a new bruise splotching the side of her left knee, and another on her right upper arm, but otherwise she was unmarked. A better day than most.

Ysbaddaden remained quiet. She looked down at his face. His features were all masculine–his wide jaw, his forceful nose. But his lips were soft, sensuous. Watching her back through slitted eyes, he gave her another of his smiles.

She must say something, anything. "I'm not the one to go against Balor." Saying the evil name, she felt stark fear, as if simply saying it aloud could make the monster appear. She struggled with her voice. "I *won't* be the one. Why don't *you* lead this battle you want?"

"I'm not a king. I have no land, no people. Where would I begin to gather my forces? It needs someone with the power, the command."

"I don't want to command. And I wasn't reared to be a queen. My brothers were meant to rule after my father, not me. I don't have the training–nor do I want it."

"But the future is already written."

"Says one Druid priestess."

"The Druids can read the stars."

"Don't you see how preposterous it is? I'll never be a match for Balor, with all the storms he can brew."

Ysbaddaden sat up, all humor gone from his face. "You will one day be High Ruler of Eire, Medb. You must accept it."

Chapter Four

Medb came back to herself, to Seamaire, to today. She drew in a sharp breath and jerked her mind away from those memories and the wing brush of shadow they inevitably brought with them.

The wind outside Seamaire's stone walls smelled of sea salt. Medb found Arawn at the side of the exercise field, leaning against a tree shedding its flowers. Since they planned to use edged swords, he wore, as Medb did, armor made of mail. He looked as strong as an ox.

Arawn wasn't alone. Goibhnui had risen early to see what kind of warrior this Queen of the Sligo made. He looked rumpled, as if he'd slept in his clothes.

Gwawl was there, too, and with him, Medb's councilors–and the folk from many miles around. Medb's face flushed with anger. So they'd all heard and gathered to observe her ordeal. She stopped before Gwawl. "How flattering of you to wake everyone so early."

He glanced sidelong at his bride. Li Ban lightly slapped her own cheek, pretending she only now realized she'd done something Medb wouldn't like. 'You didn't say it was to be a secret match."

The competition began with the usual amenities.

"We are well met, my Lord," Medb said to Arawn. "It is an honor to spar with a champion as well-reputed as you."

"Let us see how well trained you are," Arawn rumbled tersely.

Medb didn't like either his tone or his bearing. He must have reconsidered his agreement to the match overnight, and made up his mind to treat her as an apprentice, as if parrying with her were a lowering of his standards. She saw that he intended to teach her a lesson about challenging her betters.

Medb had hardly taken her stance before he came at her, all of him at once, with a high-swinging blade. Medb had feared she would be no match for him, yet she surprised herself. Skills that she'd all but forgotten came back to her; as she struggled to keep up with his offensive attack, her lack of practice told, however. The muscles in her shoulders soon ached. She wouldn't last long. She had to draw his blood quickly, or risk not only losing the match but losing the warrior, too. She gripped her sword so tightly her fingers threatened to cramp. *No–don't think about it, Medb! Just do it!* All her mind narrowed to an intense point of concentration. She made an urgent lunge into the dangerous territory within the reach of his arms. Her sword caught his from underneath, and her wrists twisted. Like magic, his swing flew wide, as Ysbaddaden's had when Skatha had shone them this technique. It gave her just enough time to whip to one side and nick Arawn's thigh, not deeply, but deep enough to draw blood.

He grunted and stepped backward, his reactions those of a mercenary. His eyes registered a flash of anger as he renewed his attack, showing little mercy from then on. When the blaze of his sword forced Medb back so suddenly that she tripped and fell, his feet straddled her, one of them coming down on her forearm. His sword point stopped just an inch from her throat.

"The battle is mine."

"Yes–I yield." With that deadly blade so near her throat, she didn't gloat about the blood that ran down his thigh.

She saw Gwawl draw his sword and step onto the field. All she needed now was for him to take offense at Arawn's stance. She lifted her free hand to cautiously push Arawn's blade aside. He gave way immediately, releasing her arm as he stepped away. He laughed just once, grimly–"Ha!"–as if at himself. As Medb rolled up to sit, he bent and gripped her arm, jerking her to her feet as if she were a straw doll. There was fury as well as courtesy in that yank.

But he held her hand for a moment, and rubbed his thumb lightly over the palm, feeling the newly risen blisters. "You have some skill, my Lady Queen, but your hands are as tender and soft as butter, and your wrists as white as snow."

Arawn was correct. The contest left her feeling

drained and slightly nauseous. And her hip hurt from her fall. She took a few steps toward the sidelines, walking painfully. She'd forgotten how hard sword work was on the body. No doubt, she'd find bruises later. And tomorrow, when she met Goibhnui in this same place, she'd be stiff. She must remember to rise an hour early, to allow time to loosen up.

Under the shade of the flowering tree, she bent at the waist to let Ehtne pull her helmet off. Straightening, she shook her hair out of her eyes. Ehtne took her sword, too, and offered her a cloth to wipe the sweat from her brow. Medb couldn't quite read the expression on her servant's face. There was surprise, and pride, and also some disquiet.

Still panting from her effort, Medb decided she mustn't prolong reminding Arawn of his wager. "It will be a pleasure to have you among my champions, my Lord."

He'd taken a cup of ale from a servant, and he made Medb wait while he poured the entire pint down his throat without taking a breath. Wiping his mouth, he looked at her, and looked around him, as if at Connaught, with smoky aloofness.

What would soothe his pride, so that he would join her service without resentment What did he want? He seemed the sort who craved honors and preferment. With that thought, Medb felt an almost imperceptible click, like a key turning a lock.

"As I told you yesterday, my man in Donegal is young and could use the advice of someone well-versed in defense."

"Donegal." He handed the empty cup back to the servant, and pulled his helmet off and gave his dark red hair a swipe. "I recall it from the old days, though my travels haven't taken me there recently. I imagine Balor must have left it in a poor way."

"He did. But it is a place rich in possibilities. And you would be my chief administrator." Medb felt a twinge of guilt. Ainle had moved his family into the citadel he'd repaired, and now he would find himself put out in favor of Arawn. But by the tone of his last report, he would greet the arrival of someone with Arawn's experience with relief. Or so she hoped.

Arawn pretended to consider her words, as if they were an proposition and not a command, as if he'd forgotten that he was honor-bound to give her his loyalty. Let him preserve his pride, she thought—as long as he surrendered in the end.

He did. "I accept your generous offer, my Lady," he rumbled, then grinned from cheek to cheek. "Since I will be your greatest servant, I'll need soldiers. A hundred good men ought to do me." His eyes gleamed with every shade and nuance of light now. She had won his oath but no reverence from him.

"I suppose I can find you that many." A warrior of Arawn's repute would attract young men looking for glory. "They won't be skilled. You'll have to train them yourself."

"I will train them and train them well, so they may hope to survive these difficult times. Then, if Treon tries our patience in Donegal, he might find himself losing his head–and some of his holdings, too."

"You aren't to provoke Treon. That's not my way."

"Why not? It's his."

"He and I are two very different rulers. *My* champions will not rile their neighbors."

"Hmm! I hope I'm allowed to defend myself, else why retain me?"

"If he provokes you, you may defend yourself–and my province–to the fullest extent of your skill. But you will not cross onto his lands without my consent."

"Then I will have to finish off any intruders he might send while they're on *my* side of the border," he answered darkly. "Let Treon try to escape and he will find that neither courage nor excellent arms can save him."

Medb found Arawn's vow daunting. Her attention was diverted, however, when Gwawl gave her a hearty slap of approval, one warrior to another. "I had no idea. Why did you keep this training with Skatha a secret?"

"There seemed no need to broadcast it," she answered irritably.

Seeing her councilors coming, smiles of wonder and pride on their faces, she knew there would be no calling the news back now.

* * *

Medb won foxy Goibhnui's oath easier than she had Arawn's. In fact, she defeated him soundly. Now she had a warrior to replace Ainle. Despite his habit of sly teasing, Goibhnui proved to be a good worker as well as a laughing, quick-handed rogue with a sword. He also showed himself to like whatever in skirts he looked upon, and his looks went everywhere. He was a handsome devil, and Medb worried for the virtue of her womenfolk. So, she put him in charge of her mining venture, off in an out-of-the-way corner of the province.

With the coming of spring, she and her folk finally had some good luck. The planting went well, and the cattle multiplied wonderfully. The provinces of Clifden and Ahascragh were equally blessed. And Arawn and Ainle reported satisfactory progress in Donegal.

To thank the Goddess for their good fortune, the people of Connaught planned a feast. Medb donated freely to the event, planned for the date when spring gave way to summer, when Imbolc became Beltene.

Early that morning, the young Druid Bran held a ceremony in the forest. In a sacred grove, he stood with his head covered by the hood of his white robe. He offered to Danu two fatted, white cows whose horns were bound together.

"Here us, Danu!" he cried to She Who Watches. "The sun shines bright on this hallowed day. The

Earth has come alive, and we are grateful." Raising his arms, Medb saw that on one he wore a circlet of wolf fur, which denoted a talent for killing, and strapped to his waist was a sickle with a golden hilt. "See us, Danu!" he shouted. "Breath in our breathe and know us as part of You!"

The folk began a chant, low and insistent. They joined hands and began to circle the Druid and the sacrificial offerings. Bran lowered his arms and threw back his hood to reveal himself to She Who Watches as he sanctified his sickle by cutting some mistletoe with it. Then he stepped toward the first animal. Setting his holy blade to the cow's throat, he said, "Accept our offering, Danu. Help the Tuatha de Dannan in our need. Render us the gift of Your favor."

Medb closed her eyes rather than watch the slitting of the poor beasts' throats. She heard Bran say, "Join with us, Danu, accept our offering, now . . . now!" His voice rang with bold urgency.

The sacrificed cows were hung on hooks to bleed, and the women boiled the blood with milk and butter from the same beasts, and flavored the mixture with savory herbs for the night's feast. Fann had recently discovered an ancient cask full of golden wine, and Medb had donated it to the celebration. Wood for bonfires was piled in an open pasture outside the burgh, the usual site of amusements and tribal gatherings. The banquet was a communal effort. Wives brought bread, girls brought cheeses, boys came from the streams with strings of trout.

As the sun disappeared, the great spring-into-summer fertility gathering began. Two great bonfires blazed to welcome the sun's warmth and brilliance and to encourage it to nurture the growth of herds and crops alike. The orange fires against the black heavens illuminated the land with an enchanted quality.

As the previously killed beef carcasses were spitted, one over each fire, Bran sang a chant of praise to Danu, blessing both the food and the company. Then the wine cask was breached, and cheers called for Medb to speak.

"I have little to say, except to thank the Goddess for providing us with what promises to be a bounteous year." She lifted her wine cup. "May our hearts keep youth and our mouths grow full of song."

A glad clamor arose. While the meat and fish cooked, the folk struck up a jubilant ballad of thanksgiving. Something inside Medb sang along. A generously proportioned woman with grown children seized the usually diffident Abrat and swung him into a reckless dance that mimicked the sun's movement through the skies. Giddiness overcame them all as the whole tribe celebrated the renewal of the primeval life force. Even Medb was drawn into the abandoned frolic around the fires. Feeling as light-hearted as a girl again, a shadow lifted from her, leaving a glow of exhilaration.

When the meat was ready, the young priest was given the first joint. Bran consumed his fill of the flesh. When he was done, the folk fell as quiet as if a spell had been cast over them. Bran sat in a trance, the meat of the god-offering working in him, allowing him to see into the sphere of the future. When he finally roused, he wouldn't say what he'd seen, however. He simply signaled the general feasting to begin and the mad dancing to go on.

Stepping in the shadows beyond the fires to catch her breath, Medb found Bran recovering from his stupor. She distrusted the prophecies made by Druids, but felt it her duty as Queen to learn what he'd foreseen.

"Many things," he said, "but foremost, I saw the shape and appearance of the one who should be made High Ruler of Eire." He looked at her keenly.

She felt the shadow fall back over her. She didn't want to ask who it was he'd seen, and almost with relief she heard mocking laughter from the field behind her. "Who is there in the rye?" she asked, annoyed. Her folk, even drunk, should know better than to trample the grain.

Bran glanced behind him. "It was the screech of a hunting owl, nothing more."

Turning her head back to the fires, Medb saw Gwawl and Li Ban ambling hand in hand. They made a comely couple. Nothing had been said yet, but Medb suspected Li Ban was with child.

"I saw into their future, too," Bran said, following

her gaze. "It is a kindly fate which veils from most folk any inkling of what lies ahead for them. Gwawl and Li Ban don't realize the long wanderings to come by your side, and the sufferings and calamity–"

"I don't want to know!" Medb cried. Turning from him, she heard that sound again, and looked into the dark. She made out faint shapes in the rye. At the same moment three torches bloomed in the field. The gaiety about the fires ended abruptly when someone called out, "Look! In the rye!"

A foul thrill went up Medb's back. And a shiver went through the gathering, splintering up the warmth from the twin fires into fragments of ice.

Small Guendoleona, whose voice was much bigger than her small frame, shouted, "Goddess be! It's a Fomor raid! Hurry, hide the children!"

As the women gathered their offspring and ran for their lodges, the men grabbed up lengths of wood for weapons and started toward the field.

They stopped short of wading into the ripening grain, however, and stood as still as the trees in the forest behind Medb. She sensed it would only take a word, and they would charge foolhardily.

One of the three Fomors sat on a fine white stallion. Gwawl pushed through to stand by Medb, facing the interloper. He glanced at her, then took another step, his hand already drawing his sword. She rushed to stop him, to hold his arm back.

"By the Goddess–let go of me! I'll hack–!"

"No, Gwawl, you will *not!*"

He looked from the mounted Fomor to her with eyes that at first blazed, then went as drab and flat as riverbed stones. Releasing his arm, she gave him a signal to stay put as she went forward to face the enemy herself.

It was Morc, a Fomor who had visited her once on the Eve of Samhain. He sat crimson-cloaked on his great white horse, holding a sparking torch over his bronze helmet. Two of his minions capered in the rye field, mocking the dancing of her folk around the bonfire, and now they touched their torches to the grain at random. Outcries from the folk at the edge of the field indicated they held back only because Gwawl held back. Their best field was going up in smoke before their eyes.

"You should have offered tribute to Lord Balor instead of Danu," said the monster before her. His ugly mouth was missing nearly all his spiked front teeth. "His feelings are hurt by your ingratitude. After all, any cause for celebration is due only to his mercy." He wore a princely bronze helmet and gold gleamed from his hands, the fastenings of his cloak, and even from the shield slung over his back. Three short javelins were tied to his saddle, each with glinting blade eighteen inches long. Even his stallion's bridle caught the fireshine like the stars above.

Medb refrained from answering him as she would like to. All she said was, "Be gone! You've accomplished your evil!"

The Fomor stayed a moment longer, but at last grinned evilly and nudged his horse. The stallion stepped away carefully, with a light, neat stride as delicate as a cat's. Only as the great animal moved did Medb see the little boy Morc led by a tether attached to an iron ring about his neck. A symbol was freshly branded on the child's forehead, showing he was his master's slave. The crowd behind Medb gasped.

"Who is that child?" she called after the Fomor.

Morc's grin grew even more cruel. "A gift from the province of Elphin."

Medb looked at the miserable boy again. Not one of her own. None of her business. Her hands made fists and she felt herself trembling with the urge to fly after the unholy beast on that fine horse, pull him down, and–

And get herself killed? Get more of her fields set afire? More children stolen? More innocents murdered?

A growl rose among the folk standing by, but Medb only clasped her arms with her hands. Morc's followers–and the child–went after him, and disappeared under the great oaks at the edge of the forest.

The fires they'd started in the rye caught rapidly, and in minutes the entire field blazed. There was no point in trying to save it. The best Medb and her sturdy tenants could do was keep it from spreading to the oats nearby. They worked all the remainder of that night, until the sun rose to set the sky afire.

The ruins of the rye crop smoldered.

None of Medb's folk would look at her. Gwawl, smoke-stained and smeared, appeared by her side and said, loudly enough to be heard, "My Lady, I apologize for acting so heedlessly. Challenging the Evil Eye's minions would have done nothing but bring even worse ruin down on our heads."

Medb knew he said this only for display. He was as angry with her as anyone, perhaps more so.

"I wish I could be as cool as you in the face of fear," he went on. "And not given to oaths to make me feel braver than I am."

Cool in the face of fear? He mocked her.

She lifted a weary hand, dismissing his false repentance, as she retired, exhausted, to her citadel. Knowing she couldn't sleep, she took up a pair of wool carders and sat by her cold hearth. There was nothing she could have done for that child except lose more lives trying to save the one.

Nonetheless, shame burned in her, and guilt. And hurt at Gwawl's interpretation of her restraint. Didn't he understand that she *hated* the helplessness of her situation? But what else could she do? Even when she tried to live peacefully under Balor's watch, it did little good. His minions struck again and again. If she were to resist him . . . she recalled too precisely the searing quality of his Evil Eye.

Nonetheless, she kept seeing Morc on that wonderful horse, the gold gleaming from every part of him–as if there were enough gold in the world to waste on such a show! What he wore to adorn himself would have bought food for her decent, quiet folk for a year.

But the Fomors had all the wealth now, and all the power. Only they had gold, only they had javelins and shields and swords to spare, and rode white stallions.

It wasn't right, it wasn't fair. A great and terrible cry wanted to break free from Medb's tightly pursed lips: Someone should–!

She didn't finish the thought, but Ceridwen's prophecy hung over her mind like a gallows at sunset.

To destroy Balor is the only way to save the tribes of Eire.

It's you, Princess; you're the one.

It rests with you, Medb.

Since the secret of Medb's training as a warrior was no secret any more, she followed Arawn's advice and exercised her fighting skills. Today she'd spent the afternoon at chariot practice, and now drove her horses through the forest toward her private place above the sea. Leaving the chariot behind, she began the long climb to the vantage point.

The sun had just set; all that lingered of the day was a smudge of peach on the western rim of the world. The evening sky above remained full of light, however, a silver light reflected by the sea.

She had come to be alone here, but Gwawl

found her. She heard his horse bring him, heard him climbing up behind her. She continued to gaze out at the wide silver panorama. Only when he'd stood behind her long enough to catch his breath did she say, "I wasn't afraid the night of the Beltene fires. I wanted to fight them as much as you did. There's nothing to be gained that way, though, and everything to be lost."

He had remained distant since that night. "Your Druid priest sought me out today."

Medb sighed. "And what did he tell you?"

"He says that in his trance he saw you as High Ruler of Eire."

Medb huffed. "It's ridiculous, isn't it? As if I could rise so high–even if I wanted to, which I don't. I think any move in that direction would be a great mistake–as you well know. If anyone knows me, it's you."

Gwawl wasn't a man of a great many words. "I don't know you at all any more."

It hurt her more than he imagined to hear him say that.

"The priest says Danu has chosen you." He labored to voice his thoughts.

"Then Danu has made a great mistake, hasn't She?"

He inhaled sharply at her sacrilege.

Medb's heart beat high in her throat. "If not Her, then these Druids. Clearly *I* am not the one to take up my sword and carve a path to the High Ruler's throne. Maybe because I *am* afraid. Certainly that poor child must think so. He couldn't have known how hard it was for me to stand there and watch that slimy creature lead him away."

Gwawl didn't comment, and she stared out at the silvered sea again. "I saw the Evil Eye wither my own father as autumn withers the leaves. I saw my mother's head placed on a pike. I saw my brothers forked like hunted prey on Conann's brutal spear." She shuddered at the memories. "I'm only trying to save others from the same fate."

"The Druid says that you know what you must do," Gwawl said stubbornly.

"I don't!" The palm of Medb's hand crept to her chest. "I am only a young woman brought to the throne by happenstance. There are others with more strength, more desire for power." The panorama of sea and sky glistened in the oblique light without her seeing it now; her mind groped in the dark. "Danu says I must gather the tribes–how can I do that without getting every man, woman, and child killed?"

She struggled for control. "No. Better to live quietly, give whatever Balor demands of us, and die in our beds of old age."

"Medb . . . it isn't working. The folk are restless, and even your soldiers are questioning your authority. If you don't do something, there may be trouble."

"What do they want? More war?"

His face flushed. "We can't lose much more by war than they're losing by this *peace* you're keeping! I'm no councilor–and certainly no queen–but even I can see that you should find out who else is left and form some alliances."

"And stir up kings like Treon?"

"Your father wouldn't have flinched–"

"I'm not my father! I have Balor watching my every move."

"Did he flinch even from Balor?"

She felt her anger deflate. "No. He stood bravely, knowing he was about to die."

Gwawl said no more. He didn't need to.

"Very well then. We'll send out more exploration parties. We'll try to establish some alliances–though little good they will do if the Evil Eye comes again in the night." She didn't look at him again, only out at the sea shimmering in the silvered summer twilight. "But make no mistake, Gwawl, I don't believe this prophecy, and I will not set myself and my folk on that road to destruction. I am *not* the one."

During the next year, Li Ban and Gwawl celebrated the birth of their first child, and Medb gained a clear picture of who lived along her borders. She sent tribute and gifts of goodwill, and received the same in return–from all except Treon and Nuada the Silver-handed, the chieftain of the Meadhe from the province of Gort. Nuada not only refused Medb's overtures of peace and friendship, but the summer after Morc burned her rye, Grainne complained to her of raids by the Meadhe on the herds in Ahascragh.

As summer gave way to autumn, Grainne's outrage demanded that Medb leave her beloved Connaught and travel to Ahascragh herself. She took an escort of ninety-two fighting men, her council members, and four covered carts laden with the goods and furnishings needed for such a journey.

Chapter Five

Cold mist and a whirling wind met them on the last day of their journey. Medb was wet and chilled through long before they arrived in Ahascragh. Though it was dark when they crossed the border, all the travelers willingly forged ahead; no one wanted to spend another night sleeping on the ground.

They came upon the sleeping houses of the town beneath Grainne's citadel with gratitude. The hill fort was built on an upland site. Grass-grown ramparts surrounded the hilltop, where Grainne's father had built a fortification of straight, upright logs.

Inside the outer wall, Grainne herself held Medb's horse as she dismounted. Trained as a bard, Grainne took such things as how to welcome one's Queen seriously. She offered the ceremonial guest cup of hot spiced wine to Medb, who put it slowly to her lips.

Medb passed it to white-haired Tochmarc. Then the cup passed on to Matth, Li Ban, Fann, and finally back into the hands of their hostess, who said formal words of welcome. That ritual performed, Grainne led them up to her tower hall and a huge, warming fire. "I'm so glad you've finally come—though I know it is a long journey from Connaught to Ahascragh these days."

Heads of beasts hung on the walls. Medb remembered visiting here as a child, climbing the great staircase to its very ramparts, playing with Grainne in a long underground dungeon, and investigating curious little flights of stairs on the palisades. Medb and she had both changed since then. Grainne had become tall and imposing. She'd studied to be a bard before stepping into her father's place here, and the training lent her an aura of grace.

She offered her queen a rich golden wine, heady and sweet, though without the spices of the guest cup. Medb quickly thawed under the drink's sun-baked flavor.

She studied the young bard's beauty. The torches on the walls knocked bright sparks out of her hair, which she wore long and straight behind her shoulders. When she spoke of Nuada and the trouble on her borders, she smoldered with rage.

"Not only cattle were stolen. Four good women were dishonored by the marauders. Two the first time, two the second." Grainne's blue-eyed gaze was dark and level. "One was a new-made bride; another a maiden, a child really, caught by surprise while hanging out her summer smocks to bleach in the sun. She is wasting away with shame. She's like a garment herself now, hung on a pole. I want revenge for her."

Tochmarc, listening to their conversation, pulled pensively at his white beard, grooming it absently. Unlike Medb, he and Matth already foresaw violence.

As soon as Medb felt rested from her journey,

Grainne feasted her. The citadel rang with laughter and the hot buzz of talk and the aromas of food and wine. And music–the music was especially good. The young, beautiful bard had an ear for song. Grainne took the harp in her hands and sang strange tunes of her own composing, as intoxicating as her golden wine. One song in particular stirred Medb; a wild call that came and came again, tingling and throbbing. It brought Ysbaddaden to her mind, his sword slicing, his muscles bulging.

Unfortunately, Nuada made another attempt on Ahascragh's cattle the very next day. The raid couldn't be seen as other than a flaunting of his sovereignty. He was all but throwing a challenge in Medb's face.

One raider was struck on the head by a herder and thereby captured. When the men carried him to Grainne, she cried out with astounding heartlessness, "Cut off his head! I'll hang it in my hall with the other wild beasts!"

But Medb ordered her folk to tend the prisoner's wounds and put him into the dungeon. She still did not want to battle Nuada, believing there must be a peaceful way to end the matter.

That very night, she dreamed vividly of Danu. The Goddess seemed fair but insubstantial, a creature of clouds and sunlight. Her handsome head was poised above glittering robes made of water and stars, Her arm raised in friendly greeting. "Medb . . . the island of Eire and its peoples have endured the curses of Balor far too long. They need their High Ruler. You are the one."

Medb wanted to deny this, but she couldn't seem to move, not even her lips.

"The road you must traverse cannot always be a peaceful one. Take up you sword, Medb, for it is the only way you can unite the tribes and rid the island of the baneful Balor once and for all. My hope, and the hope of the Tuatha de Dannan, all rest with you."

The Goddess grew more and more transparent, melting into the clouds and sunlight. Her voice grew distant. "The fate of Eire is in your hands."

Medb woke with a start. Only a dream, she told herself as she sat up in her bed, stunned and a little ill. She crept out of her bed to crouch by the hearth and its embering fire. It was only then that she saw something aglow in the corner where Ehtne had placed the chest containing her armor. She edged near the strange glowing oblong thing, almost as tall as she was herself. At last she ran her hands over it and knew it for what it was.

She met with Grainne again in the morning. "Bring me the captive Meadhe."

The warrior, called Roc, was still pale from the blow he'd suffered, yet he could stand on his own. Medb sat on her borrowed throne, trying to look noble and assured. But after last night, she felt nothing of the kind. "My Lord Roc, come closer."

The proud man stood motionless. The guards pushed him forward at spear-point, one muttering, "Show respect, prisoner! This is Queen Medb, and you'll bend your will to her or else!"

With the man before her, Medb said, "Tell me about your chieftain. I have nothing to fear from him, do I?"

No statesman, the warrior didn't realize that her scoffing tone was meant to coax out of him everything he knew about Nuada's forces and resources. Goaded by his own pride, he bragged about his ruler.

"My lord Nuada has five of the finest champions in the land, and each of them commands the finest soldiers. I myself command a hundred men, all stout hearts and gnashing teeth. Have nothing to fear from him? You have everything to fear. He has the loyalty of Daghda, famous for his heroism. And he has a third champion, a woman warrior called Finola. His Druid priest Diancecht has developed his skills at spellcasting and is a force himself to be reckoned with. And Nuada himself has his famous sword."

Medb had heard of this sword, which wasn't invincible, as Ysbaddaden's Answer was, but which had some power, nonetheless.

"You'd do well to stand clear of Gort," Roc warned. "In fact, you might consider giving King Nuada your oath of submission before he forces it from you!"

She had the satisfaction of seeing his proud bearing give way to surprise when she said, "Thank you for all this information, my Lord. You have saved me the tedium of sending scouts into Gort. You are free to go now."

"What? Free?"

"That's right. Go home to your Lord and tell him that I too am supplied with both soldiers and resources. Tell him that if he wishes to avert war between us he has just one month to send an emissary to make tribute to me in apology for his insults." She waved Roc away.

As the man's guards ushered him out of the citadel, Tochmarc said, "He won't reply, you know, not Nuada. He's too arrogant."

Medb had already guessed the truth of this. She gestured to Ehtne. In a moment the servant brought the object Medb had discovered in her room last night. It was so clearly something crafted not in this world that for a long moment no one spoke. Medb reluctantly broke the silence. "The Goddess Danu, Eire's Mother and Protector, came to me during the night." She rose to take the bright bronze from her servant. "She has blessed me with a sacred shield of vast power."

"What does it mean?" Grainne asked.

"It means," Medb said reluctantly, "that you should set your craftsmen to smelting iron and forging it into useful implements of war, for we shall soon march into Gort."

Medb didn't receive the peace offering she'd demanded from Gort, and so fell the day when she had to lead her soldiers into the province of Nuada the Silver-Handed. Grainne's Druid Catabadh accompanied her in her chariot. He was a tall, dark man, with a sly, sensual look.

Though she was no warrior, Grainne also claimed the right to lead her soldiers into battle. "I have some skill at spellcasting myself. You'll need both me and Catabadh if their Druid Diancecht is as powerful as Roc said."

Nuada's forces were caught unawares. Evidently the chieftain hadn't believed Medb would really invade. The minute her host was spotted crossing the river, however, there came an echoing blast of a horn and stark cries: "They're coming!" Women and children scurried for shelter, and warriors took up their arms.

Medb sent Grainne's forces south into the stubble-fields outside the unfortified town, while Medb, with Catabadh in her chariot, drove directly toward Nuada's citadel. The fortified rise on which it stood gave it obvious advantages, which was why she'd chosen a sudden strike. She'd hoped to find most of Nuada's warriors just as they were, outside the ramparts that embraced the hill fort.

Another harsh horn blast sent the blood tingling to her ears.

Nuada promised to make a ruthless foe, and Medb feared a savage defense from the Meadhe. But his arrogance worked against him today. The continual feuding with his neighbors had weakened his forces.

High cries rang out as a company of hastily

armed men assembled to stop the invaders at the base of the citadel. There came a ring and a clatter as both sides drew their swords. In the lead of the defenders stood Daghda, famous for his heroism. His appearance came as a surprise to Medb, for he wasn't lean and muscled as she'd expected. Indeed, in another setting he would have seemed plump and jocund. His head flamed with red hair that exploded with curl and spilled around his freckled face. More curls made a short but wild copper beard along his chin and jaw. He wore black from head to foot. Seeing Medb, he drew himself to his full height. His shield was fashioned of leather, and his iron sword shone with pale light that gleamed at the edges. She heard his rush of hoarse laughter, like a fall of sliding stones.

Amid the clamor, another deep voice lifted in command. "To the fields!"

"That's Nuada," Catabadh shouted in Medb's ear.

She caught the merest glimpse of the flat-faced ruler of the Meadhe. His eyes burning like coals, he brandished his famous sword as he headed for the field where Grainne's forces moved toward the village.

Meanwhile, Daghda and his men charged on foot toward Medb's chariot and her horse-soldiers. Bowmen atop the stone fort loosed arrows that whined and whistled past her ears. A horse went down almost beneath her chariot wheels, an arrow shot through the throat.

From the corner of her eye, she saw Catabadh thrust his hand into the rune bag tied to his belt. He pulled out several of the mysterious carved pieces, and held them in his fist as he muttered to the forces of nature. Charged power began to curl off him in waves–then Medb saw a sudden dazzling flash as bolts of eerie blue lightning streaked down from the sky into the midst of the Meadhe forces. The lightning almost blinded her, yet she saw men freeze in place, hands outspread, backs arched, mouths open in silent screams as the uncanny, glowing bolt held them rigid. When the force finally let them go, they sank to their knees and doubled over.

Medb's horses reared and tried to turn. She couldn't hold them. Her foot soldiers caught up with her now, and ran past her to meet the enemy, many of whom lay already fallen, their clothing scorched and their bodies smoking.

"I can't control the horses!"

"That's Diancecht's work. He's thrown them into confusion."

Medb too had been hit by the enemy Druid's spell, for she couldn't think. "What can I do?"

"Abandon the chariot!" Catabadh pushed her from the tossing vehicle. They both hit the ground hard, and rolled. Several seconds passed before Medb could gain her feet and look around.

She got her sword free of its sheath and raised the shield Danu had presented to her–and again she experienced a sense of controlled magic. The shield seemed to send a wave of sensation up her arm and all through her body. She felt protected and strong. She didn't have time to evaluate this impression, however, for she saw a man–rather, saw a huge arm and shoulder–swinging a glinting sword toward Catabadh as he rose from the ground beside her. For an instant she was held by her old desire for peace; then she broke free of it and leaped forward to hew at that swinging arm with all her might.

As that enemy fell back from his wound, another attacked Medb. As they exchanged blows, her sword clashed against the center knob of his swiftly presented shield and glanced aside and fell from her numbed hand. The enemy sword came at her. From nowhere, a fiery orb of molten lava plunged from the sky, striking the man about to kill her. His scream of pain shriveled Medb's soul.

Catabadh's work, she thought as she retrieved her sword. She'd never seen lava before, nor had she realized that such sorcery existed.

The sun was still climbing when she spied Daghda again, distinctive in his black garb. He was clearly cutting his way toward her. "Lady Medb, hag of all hags! Are you ready to feel my blade?" His deep snarl was at odds with his plump appearance. With a thrust of his huge hide shield, he turned away the sword of one of Medb's men, hindering his desire to get at her. He threw the man backwards to the ground and paused just long enough to stab him through the breast. And then he turned for Medb again.

How could a man walk so unconcerned through such carnage? He must be under another of the unseen Diancecht's spells. The Druid had encircled Daghda with some sort of protective force that made him seem in total command of the day.

Another of Medb's men was beset by him, and surely would have been treated to the same death already dealt to too many others, but as she saw his edged blade swing to take her soldier's head from his shoulders, a hot wrath seized her heart. She couldn't remember ever being so angry before. "Eire!" she cried, springing to the defense of her soldier. She came in under Daghda's swing and pierced him in the side with her sword.

The Meadhe champion bellowed as she pulled her weapon back. Red drops dribbled from the blade of her sword.

"That's one for Eire!" cried the soldier she'd saved.

"Our Queen's bite is deep!" another cried.

Daghda, holding his side with his left hand, didn't quite lose his pride. "You have an able blade, my Lady." As he staggered back, his forces opened around him. Medb, held by a fine, silvery trembling that took control of her entire body, felt herself hit from behind. Catabadh pushed her face-down onto the ground as arrows from her own archers came whistling over their heads. She saw three of

Daghda's men go down–but most of the arrows fell harmlessly, for that opening in the Meadhe forces kept widening.

The sun had just slid westward off its apex when came another horn blast, a rallying signal to rout the withdrawing Meadhes. Getting to her feet, Medb saw Grainne's forces joining her own. She scanned the field of battle, and saw that Nuada was also retreating. "Catabadh, send your forces around the citadel!" Medb screamed, "Don't let them get away!"

As Medb and Grainne chased down the fleeing Meadhes, Catabadh circled to meet their rush to escape. The enemy was caught between two arms of the Sligo army. A melee ensued. For some time, Medb was busy with enemy swords. The affray was sharp, but the Meadhes were unnerved by the fierceness of the Sligo offense. As Medb hewed the legs from under an opponent, she saw Catabadh slay a man double his strength. He'd performed some magic on himself, for he shone with a peculiar glamour and wielded a great sword with a glittering point.

"Throw down your arms!" Medb shouted at the Meadhes. "Throw down your arms and you will be spared!"

The besieged warriors, seeing so many of their kind fallen about them, began to drop their weapons and lift their hands in surrender. Nuada, however, tried again to flee. "Retreat!" he cried. "There is no hope for us here."

Grainne chased him down and surrounded him

with her soldiers.

Medb wiped her forehead with the back of her hand and allowed herself a surge of satisfaction before she ordered her men to gather the defeated Meadhes.

Nuada was captured, and he and his champions, Diancecht, Daghda, Roc, and Finola, were put in their own dungeon until Medb decided what to do with them.

Still thrumming with excitement, she knew she must look a wild-haired warrior woman indeed, fresh from hacking and hewing right and left. In contrast she found Grainne with her silver-blond hair drawn back neatly from her modeled features, as if she'd lounged the morning away beside her own fireside. Her graceful figure was bent over Catabadh, who, despite a nasty-looking scratch along his scalp, seemed ebullient with victory.

"They might have known better than to challenge us!"

At Medb's questioning look concerning his wound, Grainne said, "A swift duck was all that saved him."

"I felled my foe with a sturdy jab of my blade," he disagreed. "Did you see me?" he asked Medb, his sly grin back in place. Medb recalled the peculiar glamour that had radiated from him. He'd used his runes and his magic to make himself into a warrior. What else could these Druids do? Used with care, what could one so powerful as Diancecht do?

* * *

A mood of victory set the tone for the balance of that day and the next, as the conquered province was proclaimed Sligo from border to border–except for a few brawling combats that erupted between individual warriors of the merged army. When these were quelled, Medb met with her council, who had traveled from Ahascragh to advise her. Tochmarc and Matth went down into the dungeon to speak with the captives, and afterwards Tochmarc reported to Medb, "I think the lesser two Meadhe champions, Roc and Finola, can be recruited to your service, and even Daghda, but I don't know about Diancecht or Nuada."

"Those two will cause you problems," Matth agreed.

On the third day following their defeat, Medb ordered the champions brought before her, beginning with Finola, a young woman who looked rumpled and used up beyond her years. She had large green eyes, red lips, and long fair hair that fell in a wild tangle. She'd been given no time to primp or even wash since being cast into the dungeon with her male companions.

"If you will pledge me your loyalty," Medb said to her sternly, "I will open your locks and chains and see that you suffer no more indignity. I am set upon a path of peace that your chieftain interrupted, and it's my opinion that a strong defensive force is the best way to avoid aggression. For that I need champions. I offer you clemency if you'll join me and the Sligo tribe."

"A path of peace?" the young woman said wearily. "I've heard you have been chosen by Danu to unite Eire. If that is your aim, my Lady, then you will indeed need all the help you can get."

"Who told you that?"

Finola tossed her tangled honey hair and made a small face. "A priestess called Ceridwen passed through here some months ago."

Medb made a small helpless gesture. "Do you want to join me or not?"

"I accept your generous offer. As a warrior, I am still learning my discipline, but I pledge you my loyalty and my skills."

Roc also accepted her offer. His beard and drooping mustache split into a cheerfully savage grin, and his narrow blue eyes slit almost shut. "Does this mean I can eat Lady Grainne's cattle now without stealing them?"

"For that remark, I shall send you to Ahascragh to serve under Lady Grainne. Let's see how your misbegotten humor waxes when she's done with you."

"I'll put you to the most godforsaken work I can find," Grainne put in.

"And a good thing," Medb said, "for if any man needs his pride clipped back, it's you, my Lord."

Stout Daghda, given the same offer, looked Medb up and down with a smile as lazy and disagreeable as his gravel-filled voice. "I wonder what sort of life you have led, to be what you are, Queen Medb?"

When she didn't answer, he shrugged and said, "I prefer to fight for a winning tribe, even if it is ruled by a woman. I accept your offer, and vow to be true to you and yours from this hour on."

Matth and Tochmarc stood one on either side of her borrowed throne, and as he was dismissed, Tochmarc hunched forward, his shoulders tense as he pulled his white beard. "I didn't like that smile."

Medb hadn't liked it either, but at least it was a smile. "Who is next? Diancecht or Nuada?"

"The Druid first, I think," Matth said. "His runes have been taken from him, but be careful anyway. A man of his wizardry may have tricks we've never heard of."

A deceptively gentle-looking Diancecht thought her words over before he said, smiling apologetically, "May I have a drink of water, my Lady?"

Medb nodded to a servant, who hurried to offer the Druid a cup. "Will you join me?" he asked Medb. He looked at her almost sleepily, yet she imagined the air between them had thickened and shimmered. Her suspicions were roused as she accepted a cup of water herself. It never left her mind for a moment that here stood a powerful magician, a genius with the forces of nature. Though he had no runes to make his spells, who knew what talisman or totem he might have hidden on his person?

Diancecht sipped his water, and sipped again, at last saying, "Is it your intention to face Balor?"

"Rumors are rife in the land. One shouldn't take them too seriously."

"Ceridwen is hardly a rumormonger."

"Ceridwen believes what she may. What I believe is that Danu wants something I can't even understand, much less do anything about."

Diancecht took another sip from his cup of water. "Still, if a confrontation should ever come about between you and the Evil Eye, I would surely like to be there." Another sip. "I shall join you, good Queen. And praise you as the flower and fruit of divinity on earth." He smiled once more, and raised his cup to her.

She raised hers as well, seeing that he was, after all, a stupendous rascal, using a simple cup of water to daunt her.

Nuada alone of the captives was obdurate. Brought to her in chains, his beginning sentence declared war on Medb all over again. "You had no right to cross my borders! You're no better than Balor himself."

Medb thought he must be mad to speak to her in such a vein, considering his situation; yet she understood that being humiliated before his people, he yearned to save his pride.

Three days in his own dungeon had left the bones of his face standing out like bruises under his skin. Medb refrained from showing him sympathy, however. In fact, she felt so distanced from the scene that she became her own audience, observing the tragedy about to happen even as it spun itself out.

"I offer you what I have offered your champions: a place of dignity in the Sligo tribe, with the honor your skills as a warrior deserve, and the chance to redeem yourself and your name."

He glared at her. "You bring me shame and shambles and then pretend to offer me dignity?" His voice was low, but its intensity made it seem like a shout. "My dignity is my own and has nothing to do with you. Join you?" he scoffed. "I'd join Balor's nasty bunch first!"

Both Matth and Tochmarc bent down. Matth whispered, "He is neither grateful nor pleasable." And Tochmarc said, "He'll always be an adversary."

Medb knew what she had to do, and yet it gave her a sickening, sliding sensation. "It's plain that you can support no authority but your own," she said, speaking in a cool, detached voice. "I could exile you from Eire altogether."

The witnesses gasped as one.

"But I won't. I'll merely eject you from your home and leave you to roam the roads in search of another lord or lady to serve. If, true to your nature, you return to strike at my back, be prepared to die."

Nuada's former champions looked stricken.

"You will be taken to the border of Gort and Nenagh today and there released, with nothing but your famous sword and your wits. Once your feet leave the soil of this province, never set them on any province I call mine again, not if you value your life."

Nuada's mouth worked. Medb thought he meant to make some outcry, but instead, he spit at her feet. Tochmarc squawked and stepped back. Matth gestured angrily to the captive's guards. "Take him away!"

As he was dragged from the room that had once been his own hall, Nuada shouted, "You have a few skilled champions, Medb! I advise you to train them well–for your own good! For Balor will not be defeated by the surprise tactics you used on me!"

While everyone's gaze followed his voice out, Medb hardly heard him. She stared at the light of a lone candle on the table, remembering Daghda's words: I wonder what sort of life you have led, to be what you are.

Her life had led her to this. This was what she'd become. A woman with the ability to cast a man out of his own home, to make him an exile in his own land. She and Balor finally had something in common.

Conann stood uneasily before his Lord's throne, in Balor's cave-hall on Tory Island. "Medb's rule spreads almost against her feeble will. She gains more and more provinces–Kilkee, Tralee, Aran Isle, Elphin–and her power grows apace. The Finnia tribe in Cruach forced her into war last autumn.

She pleaded peace and harmony up to the last minute and still the venture ended well for her. She captured two more champions in that carnage, and managed to wed them to her cause. Weakling that she is, with nothing more than a warning that he should lead no other of his holdings against her, she released their leader Finn. So far he seems grateful–*grateful!*–for her lenience."

Balor frowned, looking past Conann into the fire that burned brightly in the central floor pit. "Lenience! These humans know nothing of conquest."

"Nonetheless, she's learned that the use of war can garner respect–though she still seems not to have convinced herself that the deaths, burnt crops, and trampled ripening harvests, are worth the gains in territory and prestige. She continues to prefer to win oaths of alliance through diplomatic means. The Elphin went to her with such an oath, knowing the Finnia were eager to absorb them."

A human slave woman eased up to Balor's throne, and poured ale from her pitcher into the cup in his hand. Conann leered at her as she backed away quickly.

"What about Treon?" Balor snapped, bringing his lieutenant back to his report.

"A more interesting sort, that one. More like us. He lives his life in broad streaks and bold colors–and is practicing a policy of aggression. His power grows at a much faster pace. He rules sixteen provinces to her twelve. More and more it becomes difficult for her to ignore him, and more and more he seems unwilling to ignore her."

Balor nodded grimly. "You're doing everything you can to set them at each other's throats?"

Conann nodded gravely. "Everything I can."

"Good. Let the rats devour their own flesh and blood down to the ends of their tails."

Conann heard a cold sound from further back in the cave, a sound as chilling as the voices of the dead.

Balor didn't notice. "Give Medb a particular warning from me, to remind her again that I rule Eire–not the Goddess."

"It shall be done, my Lord."

Medb needed no warning. Her first worry was always Balor. As she prospered, so did he, through raids on her holdings and demands for taxes.

As for her relationship with the Goddess Danu, she suffered the prophecy of Ceridwen without comment. The Goddess Mother had not visited her again, nor did Medb seek such a visit. Nonetheless, while visiting Kilkee just before the Imbolc festival at winter's end, she agreed to an early morning pilgrimage to a great circular grove of thirty-nine enormous standing stones high up in the fells. Several Druids accompanied her on foot up a snow-covered, mountain-cramped ravine. Deep drifts and slippery footings made the journey exhausting, and the frigid air burned Medb's throat and nostrils.

At last they stood at the edge of the high, stone-encircled knoll. Standing in their lee, Medb felt dwarfed by the loom of them. The priests began almost at once to discuss the mysteries of the stones, which they believed held special energy, perhaps even the spirit of a deity. Medb sighed and wiggled her toes in her boots, wondering if they were frostbitten. The wind up here cut like a boning knife. In order not to freeze in place, she started alone around the mound to inspect for herself a pair of stones with a lintel placed across their tops.

It was then that she spotted a man across the hundred-foot circle, leaning against one of the more exquisitely carved stones. Her hand went to her sword. How had he got there? The only route was the way she and her priests had come, and there had been no sign that someone had passed through the snow before them.

It was his stench that told her it was no man lounging there after all, but a Fomor.

"Lady Medb, how fortuitous to meet you here. Isn't the view immense?" He didn't look at her, but gestured to the sun just rising over the shapely hills, the mist spreading slowly among the little vales below. The birthing light reflected a raven's wings, the only motion in the otherwise still and frozen panorama.

"What do you care about the view?" She was careful not to react, not to twitch or cower.

"You're right, of course; I don't know why you and your trickster priests come here. A hilltop like this, despite these ugly rocks, is good for nothing but sheep. But then Druids are very like sheep, aren't they?"

Medb said nothing; it did no good to respond to a Fomor's grotesque and savage humor.

"And you're no better, either, are you, Medb?" he said. "Just a sheep masquerading as a wolf."

"What do you want?"

The creature slouched against the stone appeared gentle and relaxed in profile. "Why are you so unfriendly, my Lady? Hasn't Lord Balor been good to you? Your people clear the woods, grow crops, raise their stocks of cattle, sheep, and dogs, make their foul little hovels."

"Any prosperity we've achieved is in spite of your master–and in spite of the way your own kind ravages us year upon year. Whatever we have is due entirely to Danu's pleasure."

The creature turned his head, revealing a heavy, shovel-shaped face. He stood away from the stone, clicking his tongue and shaking his head. She recognized him now as Octriallach, one of the more repulsive of his kind. At his full height, however, he acquired a powerful presence.

The Fomor's large bronzed eyes, which changed now from musing reflection to focused intensity, peered out from behind long brown dreadlocks. "You are ungrateful. My Lord sees you growing proud. I bring you a message from him: 'Let her take care!' Balor says."

Medb realized in that moment just how much she'd grown away from her old desire to placate these monsters. She wanted nothing so much as to draw her sword and smite him. But he would defeat her, and then perhaps go on to slaughter the innocent Druids with her. A Fomor's temper could be arbitrary, and his anger fierce and hasty.

Bear his insults, she told herself. As he said, her people had prospered: there was enough food, the villages were growing back into towns, children didn't die of starvation and exposure anymore, nor did their parents scurry into the darkest corners at the least sound in the night. Octriallach's presence reminded her that it all could be taken away, destroyed again. She'd grown stronger, but not strong enough to foil Balor. Not nearly so strong as that.

"My Lord has heard of your ambitions. High Ruler *tsk-tsk*. But it's just an empty rank, surely."

Is it? she almost asked–almost hoped. "I've no mind to debate with you," she said, speaking only a little more quickly than usual, "or even to converse with you. What do you want? Why accost me here, of all places?"

"To remind you that you *can* be accosted any time, any place."

Medb tried not to react.

But the creature chuckled as he watched her.

"How amusing, your prim, determined air." Suddenly he stepped forward and gave her a shove that sent her sprawling, arms cartwheeling, onto her back.

"Oh!" The surprise of his action, the outrage of it, broke her self-command. Her hand reached for her sword hilt.

He stepped on her wrist, driving it into the snow. "I also bring you a message from my Lord Conann, who rides at Lord Balor's right hand. He advises you to understand that he still may make you his bride. He hasn't forgotten you."

"Go away!" Her voice was shamefully high and weak.

He knelt in the snow at her side, close enough for her to see the scars on his greenish face, like silver-gray slug trails. Close enough for her to see the rippers he had for teeth. Close enough to smell his rancid stench. "Lady Queen, I think a little humility on your part is needed in the future."

Medb ached to pull off the clothing he'd touched and scour her skin with handfuls of snow where he'd breathed on her. He saw her revulsion, and his short harsh laugh rang out darkly.

"Lady Medb!" came a half-dozen shouts behind her, and the crunch of hurrying footfalls as her priests came running. She turned her head just long enough to see them, all bundled in their warm garments. She turned back to Octriallach, not daring to take her eyes off him for more than the briefest instant–but he was gone. He'd vanished like steam, leaving nothing but the great pewter bulks of stone.

She shuddered, sick with helplessness. Any time, at any place. Balor watched her every move. And Conann . . . may Danu save her if she should ever fall under his power again.

CHAPTER SIX

As the summer days of the eighth year of Medb's rule creaked past, she acknowledged that she couldn't live in her beloved but remote seaside Connaught anymore. She put the Druid Bran permanently in charge there, and set herself to go wherever her direction or presence was needed. She started with Croom, where a scourge of snakes were destroying the cattle. The Fomor Ruadan visited Medb to tell her he'd loosed the vipers. "Your people hid their cattle from the tax collectors last Samhain's Eve. If they'd given Lord Balor the cattle, they wouldn't be dying now."

If Balor was so incensed at the Sligo's growing power, she wondered what he was visiting upon the Sidhe Fuait, who were growing much faster. Treon must gallop from madness and back by Fomor blights.

She'd brought Diancecht south to Croom with her. As her most powerful Druid, he was working night and day to both heal the poisoned cattle and slay the serpents.

She also had her ever-loyal council with her, and where Li Ban went, Gwawl went, too, since she had recently announced that she expected their third child. Gwawl would not let her travel without him though the baby would not be born until spring.

Medb realized she might have to move her cortege again soon, for there had been a cattle raid in Moate, and Senchan, Medb's ally there, was afraid Treon meant to declare war. Senchan was old and sickly and barely left his bed anymore. He didn't have the strength to defend himself.

Lately, Treon made no secret of his own aim to be High Ruler. He'd put out a call for champions, inviting "all who would give their lives for freedom." He'd formed a grand cavalry of pure white stallions, a thing sure to attract warriors hungry for glory. Though his tribe prospered, he was not beloved by his neighbors, for he was following a clear plan of conquest.

Accordingly, the raid into Moate wasn't about cattle, which he had in great numbers; it was a test of Medb's borders–and her mettle. Treon would have loved to control Moate and exploit the great silver mines there.

As the season of Lughnasad advanced toward another Eve of Samhain, Medb received a diplomatic visit from Cowynn, Treon's Druid priestess.

"I bid you welcome, my Lady Messenger," said Medb from the throne of Croom's citadel. "You honor my roof with your company."

"I thank you, my Lady Queen," Cowynn said in a treble voice. She was a woman with considerable poise despite her youth. Standing in a dance of autumn sunlight coming through the open hall doors, she bowed deeply, then clasped her hands before her face and extended them in the benediction of a Druid priestess. Her journey beneath the late summer's scraped white sky had left her with a sunburned face. She'd come well-dressed, however, in a cloak of green with a crimson bodice and skirt beneath. Her hair was a cap of rough silver yellow adorned with three dragon stones. Treon had dressed her to make an impression.

"You are most kind to greet me so pleasantly," she said, "considering the recent trouble in Moate. My Lord Treon dispatched me to make his apologies, and to offer tribute for any damage or deaths caused by the outlaws." She unwrapped a cloth package to show a bronze neck ring, known as a torc. "Please accept this gift, and may it grace your comely features and royal form."

The torc was carved with plants and animals in highly intricate patterns. The two open ends were rendered into the heads of fish. "It's quite beautiful," Medb said, examining it. "Thank you. Tell King Treon I shall treasure it as I treasure peace."

But she wasn't finished with Cowynn. "You used the word 'outlaws.' Yet I'm told the raid was led by none other than Karllyl, a warrior in Treon's service, and Darvyd, King Treon's bard."

"Lady, the clever fellows were indeed dressed as Karllyl and Darvyd. It was an attempt by a devious faction in Laois to take your cattle while making war between my Lord and you. King Treon is considering retribution against Ilbreach for his actions against you."

Medb saw the ploy now. Treon, as greedy as ever, had sent his men to test Moate. Finding Medb's forces there too great for him, he could still blame the foray on Ilbreach in Laois, giving him an excuse to attack that tribe and add yet another jewel to his growing necklace of conquered provinces. It would also bare Moate's borders on three sides to Sidhe Fuait attack.

She said none of this to Cowynn, of course. Instead, she turned to her faithful servant Ehtne. "Prepare mulled wine for our esteemed visitor."

The young Druid bowed deeply again. "Lady, you are most kind."

Medb rose from the throne. "Come, sit with me by the fireside where we can discuss our concerns in greater comfort."

Considering the mildness of the day, the fire was only a convenience. Ehtne heated the wine on it, and Cowynn approved her cup. "Very pleasant."

"I trust the season finds your Lord well?"

"Lord Treon is well. Indeed, he prospers everywhere, and basks in Danu's blessings."

"I hear he is set on becoming High Ruler."

Cowynn shrugged. "He is set on freeing Eire. But there are many who love him and would gladly see him rise that high."

Love him? Medb hardly thought so. No more than this dainty-looking Druid was loved, for in serving Treon she'd become a priestess of little honor.

"There is a rumor that you wish to be High Ruler yourself, my Lady."

"Not I," answered Medb. "I merely do what I can for the benefit of my people."

"Yet there is a rumor that Lady Ceridwen–"

"A rumor that circulates without my pleasure."

The Druid nodded sympathetically. "Though you have done well in your position–indeed, have been extremely brave for a woman–yet in the end, no woman can be the equivalent of a man. Naturally, you prefer an end to the difficulties of your unnatural station."

"My station feels natural enough, woman or not."

"Yet you must crave the delights instinctive to our sex–hearth and home, security and peace. Family. Children. I have seen the wildest of girls find calm in having their first child."

"You are young; you can't have seen much of anything yet. But even if I did care for such things, they don't seem fated for me. I am a queen whether I wish it or not, and so long as I am, I shall perform as one."

The Druid drank her wine, and studied the fire, and took her time before she spoke again. "I wonder, my Lady, if you could not have both the pleasures of power and of marriage."

Medb stiffened, sensing something of what was coming.

"Lord Treon has entrusted me to tell you of his

heartfelt sorrow that your marriage did not take place that fateful night so many years ago. As you know, he has not wed, either. He has kept his heart free, always hoping that the marriage may yet occur. He told me, 'I love my own folk above all things, but ever and again a longing grasps me for the maiden I was to wed.' I believe the ocean itself is not so strong as the waves of his longing."

Medb raised her brows. "This comes as a great surprise. He's never indicated that he cared whether I lived or died."

"Oh yes." The lie slid smoothly from between her callow lips. "Through all these years of confusion since that heinous time, he's never forgotten you."

Medb felt a rush of exasperation. She reminded herself that this was no different from any other invention of diplomacy, one of those lies laid out during the delicate process of dealing with another tribe. She said, "Our betrothal was set aside, and between then and now much has happened, not the least my father's death." She repressed a shudder, recalling briefly that moment when Balor opened his evil eye and stared at Aed.

But Cowynn wouldn't let the matter slip away. "Yet there could be considerable benefit to both you and Lord Treon in an renewal of that betrothal. You have several provinces under your rule, and Lord Treon has several more."

Four more, Medb thought, all gained through violence, without even an attempt at a peaceful alliance.

"With you at his side, and your provinces numbered with his, my Lord could easily achieve the position of High Ruler, and thereby do much good for Eire. You could both gain power–and domestic happiness. He loves you. Would you be so brutal as to deny him? It is well known that you were his first choice."

"I hardly think–"

"The fact is, my Lord considers your betrothal to him still valid. Your father is sadly gone, and all your brothers, but he doesn't believe that nullifies the agreement. Indeed, it makes him feel all the more his responsibility for you. As your rightful guardian and advisor, he feels that the time has come for you to relinquish to him the burdens you carry on your shoulders. 'Put aside these unfeminine duties,' he directed me to say to you, 'and honor now the marriage arranged by your beloved father.'

"He knows," she went on in the face of Medb's aghast silence, "that it won't be easy for a woman of your character to shed the cares of leadership, but he assures you a place at his council table whenever the good of your former provinces is considered. Since you said yourself it wasn't your wish to be a queen and that you wear your crown only out of duty then it will surely relieve you mightily to hand over your authority to a man whose objective is for the common good of everyone–the unification of Eire."

Medb took the time to inhale slowly and deeply before she began her answer. "First, I do not regard myself betrothed to Treon." Her voice was small, clear, and deadly. "Tell your Lord that he forfeited any claim to me in his hurry to mount his horse and run away from Seamaire, with all his men, leaving the Sligo to fight Balor alone. Leaving me to be carried away by Conann. He showed his true nature then, which is that of a coward."

Into this lake of hostility, Cowynn ventured cautiously, "My Lady, I have surprised you with my Lord's message. You will, of course, want to take some time–"

"I need no time for this folly! Treon's audacity to think he can call himself my guardian, or anything but a villain and a liar, galls and goads me to a rage you'd best not wade into deeper, Cowynn. To send you to trifle with me like this, to even consider that I would fall in tamely with his grasping ambitions and devouring intrigues . . . !" Medb found herself at a loss for words.

She stood. "Tell him these are my answers–as a woman, as Queen of the Sligo, as a commander who knows something of the art of war. Tell him he will stay clear of my borders–*or he will learn what this mere woman knows of bloodshed and slaughter!*"

The Fomors in Conann's hall laughed and shouted. One made groping movements with his hands, as if cupping large female breasts and fondling them–what he'd like to do to the human slave girl dancing to the music of a drum. Ethnui sat at Conann's feet watching the wild dance that had terror at its heart. She'd brought the girl to Conann as a gift. She was the daughter of a Druid chieftain who had dared challenge Ethnui rather that pay his taxes. After clubbing him soundly, Ethnui took forty-six of his cattle, fifteen hundred weight of grain, and his daughter.

The girl was only fifteen, yet she carried herself like a queen, not slumped down into her hips but well-supported in the small of her back. Born to dance. And being human, born to be a slave. Conann would ravish her tonight. Envisioning what he would do to the girl made Ethnui shiver with delight.

Judging by the drool stringing from her master's lower lip, Ethnui knew he was envisioning it, too. She took advantage of his rarely pleasant mood to say, slowly, as if only pondering aloud, "I hear Treon has put out a call for champions, claiming he's going to crown himself High Ruler."

Conann licked his lips and made a curt gesture. "Bah! That showy daredevil."

She had to be careful. He sometimes took offense at her reports, even though he insisted on hearing them and would have her feet roasted if she wasn't prompt in delivering them. Or punish her with his tooth-studded whip as he had once before. She gave him a sidelong glance of adoration before she went on in the same negligent way. "The whole country is in a smolder." She raised her voice only enough to make her words clear in the din. "What if Treon gets the champions he needs?"

One corner of Conann's mouth drew back strongly, forming a crease in his scarred cheek. "What if he does, that dark-eyed monkey?"

"If he unites the tribes, they may try to rebel against us." She felt edgy, excited.

"And we would get the chance to sharpen our blades on human bones again, and dip our spears in crimson. About time, I say." He reached for the ewer to refill his cup. The firelight brought out the deep, blood-red passion of the wine he poured. The drum music endlessly throbbed, beat, moved, as compelling as the procession of a sacrificial offering–which it was.

Ethnui spoke again. "Does Lord Balor know that Treon has grown so bold? If he defeats Medb–"

"By the dogs of hell! Let the vermin do what they will!" Conann slammed his fist against the arm of his chair, his peace of mind torn open at last.

"But they never gather head, these risings," Ethnui hurried to say. "But if one did, they'd get what they deserve for their base ingratitude."

Conann grunted and raised one hand to his scar. He had a habit of stroking it when annoyed, as if the feel of it soothed him. The drums continued their pour of sheer noise, and gradually, his face returned to its lustful blank as he watched the little human cavort.

The dance ended, as all dances must, and in the dead silence left by the suddenly stilled drums, Conann shouted, "Come here, maid!" When the girl balked, he gave a shout of enormous laughter, stood violently, and lunged to seize her.

With Cowynn's mission come to naught, and her further presence unwelcome, she wisely departed Croom before the noonday of her arrival was past. Treon's effrontery, however, cut Medb like a tooth-edged saw long into the night. For him to think her such a fool! To suggest he had any authority over her! How dare he . . .

Her thoughts turned and turned on these points as she paced her bedchamber. Late in the night, she fell back into her bedbox exhausted, yet sleep brought only vivid nightmares.

The following day she spoke with her council about the situation. "I think that if I can establish my presence in Moate and talk to Ilbreach in time, I can gain his allegiance before Treon invades him."

"It's an unlikely maneuver, given wavering." Li Ban sat placidly, her hands folded on the shelf of her slowly ripening belly.

"But it could show Treon that if he tests us this way, he's not apt to be pleased with the result," Matth said.

Tochmarc agreed. "You ought to go, my Lady, and you ought to go soon."

Speed was imperative. Treon had shrewd eyes

and a sharp little mind; as soon as he heard her answer to his "proposal," he would storm Ilbreach's forces, and Medb couldn't protect Laois then. She might even lose Moate too.

Her swift moving ebony horse gave a tight little whinny as she mounted into her saddle not an hour later. Ehtne had a flushed, mulish expression on her face. She didn't like Medb to go anywhere without her.

"I've heard something that needs looking into," Medb called down to her. "But we won't be parted for long. Gwawl will bring you and the others to join me as soon as you can pack."

"Ah, yes," muttered the serving woman, "we'll be along–to the sunny palace of Mag Brom."

The comment allowed Medb to depart with a smile. Ehtne was a careful housekeeper, and Senchan's citadel in Moate was not impressive for its tidiness.

Medb's escort guarded her closely as she traveled a grassy river-side path eastward. As her horse's motion grew hypnotic, her sleepless night began to tell. Marriage. Would Ysbaddaden have wed her–if she hadn't rebuffed him by the way she'd left Ben Skellig? Her eyes drooped and her mind saw again that faded time. The light changed all around her and she wandered back through the grown up years to the months she'd spend in Skatha's tiny peninsula kingdom.

Under Skatha's tutelage, Medb had grown into a competent, but not a great, swordswoman. Skatha admitted this with some apprehension. They stood under a yew tree out of the pounding sunlight, with the sound of the sea lapping Ben Skellig's shores. "Perhaps we have harbored too small an ambition for you," Skatha said. "It must be that Danu means for you to gather people, not conquer them. She's chosen you not for your strength or skill with a sword, but for an ability to rally and hold the folk to a cause. If your gifts are not of the arm, they must be of the head, or the heart." Her reasoning seemed to satisfy her. "If you can make them love you, Medb, they will follow you to the ends of Eire if need be."

Ysbaddaden seemed to hear only half this logic. "Aye, you rally them and *I'll* be your sword arm. Fate has pitted us both against Balor. With your leadership and my hardy blade, we'll erase his very presence from Eire."

But she wanted no part of either plan. She simply wanted to go home and forget Ceridwen's prophecy, to live quietly, perhaps bring back some order to her father's despoiled and destroyed provinces. That was the limit of her ambition.

Ysbaddaden continued to badger her, and her happiness became brittle with their differing ideas and downright quarrels. He was all for going home with her, to begin immediately to unite the tribes by any means necessary.

She grew reluctant to discuss her plans with him, and one day she made up her mind to leave secretly, under cover of night–and leave him behind.

Her decision meant that she mustn't care for him anymore. But how to turn aside those young feelings that galloped forward like a chariot out of control? Nonetheless, she threw herself off that racing chariot; she let Ysbaddaden speed on without her.

Their last hour together came when he coaxed her to walk by the sea with him in the blue of an evening fast deepening to violet. A crescent moon rose, shimmering on the surface of the sea, as still as a sword on the knees of a sleeping sentry. Ysbaddaden took Medb's hand and said her name in a dark, sweet voice. "Medb."

She gave him a darting glance, and by his expression she knew that in that single word he had come as close to declaring himself as a man of his steel ever could. Her heart beat wildly. She didn't know how to quiet it–because she knew she was going away from him, going where she wouldn't hear his laugh, nor his deep, teasing voice, nor see his swaggering shoulders or his mocking glance. She felt as though all the blood in her body were turning to tears. And she knew that if she couldn't care for him, she could never care for anybody, ever.

Medb came back to the cold-gleaming day at hand as her horse skittered, frightened by a girl coming along the river path with a gurgling pitcher on her hip. Her party was riding beneath elms that twined in bare, branching lacework overhead. Their horses' hooves squelched the thick, sopping leaves beneath the trees. The girl stood aside as they passed, and hailed them timidly, "Where are you going, strangers?"

Goibhnui answered the girl. "Queen Medb travels east to Moate."

There was a small silence, like a drawn breath. Then the girl exhaled, "Ohhh."

Medb glanced back at him and he smiled his lazy, feral smile, like a handsome animal snarling. She shook her head herself at his mischief. At first she hadn't liked Goibhnui, hadn't treated him with the affectionate jibing she accorded her other warriors, but merely tolerated him, until he'd helped her out of a tight spot in a battle to keep Aran Isle.

Ainle, still boyish-looking after all these years, rode to her right. She'd called him away from Donegal to join her personal guard some months ago. To her left, Daghda returned her glance and went on humming loudly. His blue eyes crinkled in their nests of freckled flesh.

She shook off her drowse and tried to take an interest in the road. The sun-dappled late morning flowed on and those memories of Ysbaddaden beckoned again. She mustn't remember. It did no good. Though there were reports that he'd offered his sword to many a ruler, he'd never so much as stepped across a border belonging to her. He'd taken her desertion hard, and ever since, he'd been searching for another ruler to satisfy his ambitions.

Medb knew that if they ever met, it would likely be as enemies. Yet . . . if she couldn't care for him, she could never care for anybody.

In the long shadows of an icy evening, a tall and powerfully built warrior clambered up through the trees and scrub vegetation and old rock-bones of an ancient hill. The path was rugged and stony, and he fared slowly, startling a stag and two kittiwakes. Since he'd grown distrustful of his fellow man, he preferred to travel his own path and not those used by others; the autumnal flights of the birds had guided him here.

As he crested the hill, he looked down on Strabane. He'd been weeks getting here, but his arrival didn't hearten him. Once he had been a hopeful young man, but much had happened to him between times, things that had finally opened a dark door within him.

He made his slow way down the lee of the stony hill. A cold dusk wind arose. Ducks raised a cry as he passed a watery pool at the hill's base. He came upon a herdsman goading his cattle home for the night. "Hail, friend!" he called in his deep voice. "I am Ysbaddaden, a warrior for Eire. Does King Treon offer shelter for such as me in this place?"

The herdsman, taken by surprise, was a good deal disturbed. The square-jawed, blunt-faced man stared at Ysbaddaden with gaping eyes. He pointed north. "Our King has a tent for adventurers. You'd be welcome there."

Nodding his thanks, Ysbaddaden started on. The herdsman called after him, "Are you really the great Ysbaddaden?"

"I am Ysbaddaden," he called, without looking back; "'great' is a word for bards."

He had been given hospitality in many a province over the years, but Treon's was among the best: a stout tent, a little carved wood bedbox with few bugs in the mattress, a servant ready to bring him hot water to wash off the dust of his journey, and bread and soup from a bubbling cauldron, spiced and flavored. He unburdened himself of his pack and armor, and his sheathed sword, Answerer.

He wasn't surprised when, finished with his meal, Treon himself appeared at the tent door. "May I enter, warrior?" He was the same stocky, bearded man Ysbaddaden recalled from the night Medb was almost married to him. He had the same sharp-eyed, intent manner–though it wasn't quite so shrill anymore. He'd become more indisputably a king, radiating arrogance and command.

Ysbaddaden nodded curtly, standing in respect of the man's rank as he entered. The King of the Sidhe Fuait brought in some of the cold, clear air of the night with him. He sat at the table, in the envelope of light and warmth from the lamp, and gestured for Ysbaddaden to resume his seat as well. The lamplight wrapped them both in privacy.

"I hear you are a warrior of great skill." Treon's

eyes shifted to the sheath that encased Answerer.

"And I hear that you intend to become High Ruler of the Tuatha de Danann."

Treon smiled politely. "You are a forthright man."

"I am a man who has searched long for a leader able to lead the children of Danu against Balor."

"Do you think I might be that leader?"

"I don't know. The last time I saw you, you were leaping on your horse, calling for your men-at-arms to forsake Connaught to Balor."

Treon's eyes didn't waver. "And what should I have done? Stayed and been murdered like Aed? When a battle is lost, the good commander makes a strategic retreat–and lives to fight another day."

Ysbaddaden recalled that at the time it hadn't seemed so much strategic as cowardly. The man hadn't even stopped to rescue his betrothed.

Yet Treon was his last hope. The King of the Sidhe Fuait had gathered nearly half the provinces of Eire under one banner; he'd had enough fortitude for that–or enough greed. Ysbaddaden didn't care anymore which sentiment drove him, as long as it was strong enough to drive him all the way to Tory Island. That was what Ysbaddaden had come to see for himself: Did Treon mean to become High Ruler only to strike some bargain with Balor for the continued enslavement of Eire, or did he mean to do more than that?

"Rumor says your quest isn't just another fire without fuel. I'm not interested in fighting for another king intent only on swelling his power just short of attracting Balor's attention."

"You speak lightly of what is a serious matter. Have you no fear of the Evil Eye?"

"I'd be a fool if I didn't–and I am no fool." He'd seen the monster shrivel King Aed with one glance of his heinous gaze. He knew as well as anyone that attracting Balor's attention was the equivalent of drawing down a gathering storm, one that might well end in a limitless darkness for the folk of Eire. But he impatiently dismissed such thoughts. "I believe the monster can be defeated, and Conann with him, and all their Fomors driven back into the shadow world so that Eire can be free again."

"This is dangerous talk. Many a man would die in such a venture. And everyone would pay the penalty for failure."

"The life of every man is bound to death, and relieved only by an agreeable story." He forced a small, cool smile. "Worse is living long without honor. When I took up my sword, Answerer, I swore to the Goddess to defeat the evil that rides our souls like a horseman. Therefore my destiny is preordained, with death at its hub."

Treon considered him thoughtfully. "You and I seem cut of the same cloth."

Ysbaddaden remained cautious. "What is your plan?"

"Immediately? I am in something of a hurry to move down into Laois and unite the good farmer-king Ilbreach to the Sidhe Fuait tribe."

"And after that? Will you bring the Sligo under your banner next?" If Treon really was intent on the crown of the High Ruler, he must defeat the Sligo. Ysbaddaden awaited his reply.

Treon smiled flames. "Medb rules twelve provinces to my sixteen. There is no other ruler who controls more than four. With her tribe behind me, I would surely win the crown."

"What says Medb of this?" Ysbaddaden controlled his voice. It wouldn't do for his emotions to show.

"I recently sent her tribute and the advice that she voluntarily join her power to mine." Treon made a gesture. "Honor demanded I show her that much courtesy. But she refused–and treated my envoy woefully in the bargain. Once I defeat Ilbreach, I'll have too much power for her to spurn me again–especially if I have Eire's finest warrior among my champions."

Ysbaddaden ignored the flattery. He knew what he was; he'd been proving it against the hardness of the world for nine years. He did what he was good at, then did it again on the morrow. Every petty chieftain and king in Eire had at one time or another tried to recruit him. He'd given his trust to some, only to be disillusioned, for he held fast to his desire to find a ruler with the courage to face Balor. For this he'd wandered the land in loneliness since the day he'd left Ben Skellig.

"It's said you once trained with Medb, with Skatha as your teacher."

A puff of wind found its way under the tent door and set the lamplight to shivering. "I knew Medb, yes." *She wormed her way like a maggot into my heart and then forsook me, and for that I'll never forgive her.*

Treon was watching his face. Ysbaddaden detected a small prick of curiosity in Medb's former bridegroom–and a strong hunger. What did he hunger for? Not Medb. Her provinces, of course.

"Could you fight against her?" the king asked.

"For Eire, I will fight anyone who stands in the way of a combined campaign against Balor. Medb hasn't the boldness for that. She never did."

"She has proven herself fierce in battle. She has battered such warriors as Nuada and Finn as naturally as a mother slaps her sons. And she is the commander of many heroes. Some even believe she is destined to be High Ruler, chosen by the Divine Danu herself."

"Backed to a wall, she apparently can do wondrous deeds, but she will never willingly face Balor, or even the weakest Fomor. From what I hear, she'd let them tax the people to starvation and turn their meadows into marshes and uproot their forests tree by tree rather than stand up to them."

"Do I detect some grudge against the great Queen of the Sligo?"

"No grudge," he lied, "just a true estimation of her courage. Though she has accumulated some loyalties, she will never do what needs to be done. She is one of those who stand in the way."

Treon nodded slowly, shrewdly. Ysbaddaden sensed that he'd revealed too much. "If I were to give you my allegiance, would you do what needs to be done?"

There was a set to Treon's lips, and a cold, squinty hardness to his eyes. "You wouldn't regret joining me, warrior."

Ysbaddaden was not completely satisfied by this answer, but he knew that most people shied from speaking as boldly as he did. "Very well, then. I am yours, my Lord King."

Chapter Seven

Alone again in the tent, Ysbaddaden sat on his bedbox. The candle cast shifting shadows on the tent cloth, encouraging his shifting thoughts.

He had been dazzled by Medb from the moment he'd first seen her that night her father meant to wed her to Treon. When she'd thrown back her veils to see what everyone was peering at through the fog, he had ignored the oncoming balls of torch light, because he'd been blinded by the loveliness and grace of her. The trace of tears on her cheeks touched him beyond belief. And when Conann carried her off, outrage rose up in him like a rearing stallion. He ran after Balor's hordes and, by Danu's blessing, found a way to save her. He still remembered how she'd regained consciousness lying there on the ground, how her eyes had rolled around to look at him like a wounded doe.

She seemed far above his reach, however. She was a princess, with a mouth as red as a ripe strawberry, feet small and light, a body smooth and slender, hair that fell in buckles of gold. During the journey to Ben Skellig, and even as they trained under Skatha, he tried to keep his admiration hidden. But it would assert itself, for he was a man and she a woman, and nature will take its course.

He felt such excitement over Ceridwen's prophecy. It baffled him when Medb refused to acknowledge it. He tried to understand that she was still young, that she had been thrust violently out of her family into the world. He told himself that she would come around when need commanded it; when the time was right she would embrace her destiny. Yet it troubled him that she couldn't do it *now.* He knew he shouldn't press her, but he couldn't stop himself.

On a night when a crescent moon rose above the sea, casting a prickling of light on the dark skin of the water, he tried to make all his feelings clear. He wanted to take her in his arms, but all he could do was say her name.

In return, she said, "I've never thanked you for what you did."

"What was that?"

"You saved my life."

"Oh." He thought for a moment, then added, "I was more afraid the monster might keep you alive."

She shuddered. "I owe you so much, and I can never repay you."

"You can."

"I can't, my friend."

By her tone, he realized that she was sorrowing. "What–?"

She placed the tips of her fingers over his mouth. "I can't, Ysbaddaden, and it breaks my heart to know that soon you're going to think badly of me."

What did she mean? Why was she speaking as

though there would never be another chance for her to say what she wanted to say?

"I hope you'll remember our friendship when all the resentment burns away."

What was this about? He refused to be alarmed by it. "You speak so strangely, as though we won't meet again on the morrow, and the morrow after that."

"One never knows the changes and chances of this mortal life." Suddenly she came up on tiptoe–and kissed him quickly–then broke away and ran for Skatha's citadel.

Ysbaddaden knew he would find no sleep in his chamber there. He always felt more at ease under the sky than under a roof, so he remained on the beach. She'd kissed him! Did that mean she cared for him? Would she wed him? Would he ever find the courage to ask her? Would he ever find the way to give her the will she needed to unite Eire?

He sat wrapped in his cloak, wondering how any girl had gotten such a grip on him. But Medb wasn't any girl; she was as polished and edged as a stiletto, and she'd slid between his ribs right into his heart.

He lay back, and even fell asleep for a while. When he woke, he drowsily watched the crescent moon set and the sky darken to that hour before dawn which is the blackest. Now he remembered more of their exchange than simply the kiss she had given him. Why had she run from him like that? Why had she spoken as if they might never meet again? Those questions echoed in his heart. For the first time in his life, he wished he were more adept at dealing with emotions.

Then suddenly a glimmer of what she'd been trying to say came through, along with an urgent sense of being too late. The birds had begun their first faint melodies, and the dawn light was turning the sea an ashen rose as he stood. That shining, stirring daybreak didn't hearten him, for his sense of belatedness grew. He started back for the citadel, unable to calm his thoughts. His mind chased around and around like a mouse in a trap, chasing things Medb had said and not said.

He hurried back through the first flood of the golden morning sun to find Skatha sitting alone in her hall, on a bench before her fire. As he came in, she turned to look over her shoulder at him. Her expression made him falter. He rapped out, a little breathlessly, "I must talk to Medb."

The fire illuminated Skatha's light copper hair, turning it to flame. "Come sit with me, Ysbaddaden." She shifted on the bench, making room for him.

But her manner warned him. Instantly he knew, though he didn't want to know. And didn't want to feel that unwarrior-like terror.

She patted the bench. He walked toward her, reluctance in every step. Closer, he saw that her face was pale.

He didn't take the seat she offered. "She's gone, isn't she?"

Skatha looked up at him and nodded. Tears stood in her eyes like diamonds, sharp enough to draw blood.

"Will you train me without her?"

"Of course, to the extent of your ability–or to the extent of mine, which I'm sure we'll reach sooner."

He nodded once, and turned to get his sword.

"Ysbaddaden." Skatha's voice trailed after him. "She left that . . . for you."

He saw what she meant, on the table, exactly where Ceridwen had first placed it. Answerer. He strode to it, and pulled it free of its sheath. The blue jewel in its hilt glowed; the sharp edges of its blade glinted. He'd never dared to touch it before. Now he felt the power of the weapon's magic surge up his arm. He swung it at an invisible foe, and it left a bright tracery in the air.

And all the time he tried to behave as if nothing mattered but learning to wield this sword of revenge. Medb was gone. *Gone.* The sensations of magic and misery combined to make him slightly mad: None of this was happening. None of it had ever happened. Presently he would awaken from a months-long stupor induced by some accident, some lightning-clap or fallen rock or flailing horse-hoof that had dissolved the crucial thread and let him fall into madness for a while.

Then came the pain, in all its molten terror. He leaned against the table, dizzy and sick, his pulse thundering in his ears. He heard the hall door open, heard light, womanly steps enter. He opened his eyes, praying to see Medb standing inside the door, eyeing him quizzically, wondering if he was having a fit.

He looked. She wasn't there. The door remained closed. No one had come in.

She was gone.

In the carved wood bedbox in Treon's tent, Ysbaddaden sat with his head in his hands. Fatigue washed over him like stagnant water, and he rubbed his face wearily. His feelings for Medb remained strong even in the midst of his resentment of her. He knew enough of those two emotions by now to understand that they would never burn themselves out. But his feelings weren't important. What was important was that Treon seemed ruthless enough to unite the tribes of Eire. If he didn't take his cause further than that, at least it was much more than anyone else was willing to do.

Aye, for Eire he could fight Medb.

Yet the thought struck a chill deep in his spirit.

He rose. Standing at the door of the tent, he could just make out the untidy huddle of wooden structures that made up the burgh beneath Treon's fortress. His citadel stood like an eagle brooding over a nest of sparrows. Treon hadn't fooled him; the man still acted only for himself. He hadn't changed. But neither had Ysbaddaden. He still believed that somehow he could force others to do what he knew they *should* do.

* * *

Medb made her hurried journey to Moate without incident until the last encampment before crossing the border. While her men set up their tents, she took on the task of watering the company's horses, mainly because she craved a few moments alone. It drained her to be in the company of men so much, enveloped in their raw, masculine vitality and power. She didn't fault her escorts for what they were; indeed, it was because they were altogether men, and altogether of their time and place, that she had chosen them. But now and again she needed a few minutes alone.

She took the opportunity to remove her sword, tug up her skirt, and pull off her woolen hose to wade into the chuckling river. The cold numbed her saddle-weary legs.

Something told her to glance over her shoulder. Some nagging marginal awareness that things weren't as they should be. She saw her watering horses, and saw several of them abruptly tossing their heads, a signal she wasn't alone anymore. She let her eyes drift along the trees of the riverbank. Everything felt wrong suddenly. And her heart turned over to see a stranger cloaked in gray at the edge of a copse. She sucked down a gasp. The slanted, late-afternoon light and the long shadows made it hard to identify him. She saw separate details only: long blond hair, an azure headband, a frowning expression on a narrow face. His hand lingered on the hilt of his belt dagger; indeed, his whole aspect seemed menacing. She glanced at her sword, lying with her hose on the riverbank.

"Hardly wise," the stranger said.

A splash behind her, beside her, a scattering of icy water that made her call out in fright as a strange horse swashed through the shallow river so near her it almost knocked her down. The animal gained the opposite bank, trotted past the stranger and vanished in the copse behind him. Or into some shadow place.

An outlaw? Something worse? Nothing seemed right about either him or his horse.

"I've come only to warn you to forget the prophecy of Ceridwen. Danu has lost faith in you. Treon is now Her choice for High Ruler. Cross swords with him and you are damned."

Medb could put no quality to the voice, whether it sounded young or old. But it hinted at an elusive force of personality, a force to be reckoned with. She still couldn't make out clearly what he looked like in that shadow, which wasn't all that deep, or shouldn't be. Some deceit of leaves and sun disguised him there.

It came to her: here was a true Sidhe, one of the fey folk who were the ancestors of the three Sidhe tribes. A swimming feeling came over her. She anchored herself to what was real. She said, as staunchly as she could, "You are the Druid Lleflys."

"Call me what you will. My true name is not for

using. I use the religion when it serves my needs, but there is an older knowledge than Druidism. I've come to tell you I've foreseen Treon holding the Lia Fail." The Lia Fail was a legendary talisman of great power, given by Danu to the High Ruler of her choice. "For your sake, Queen Medb, do not put faith in Ceridwen's prophecy anymore. Bend to Danu's new choice."

"I put faith in no seer's prophecy." She managed to sound terse and annoyed.

"Then you will not war with Treon?"

"I will stand between my folk and Treon's greed."

"Then nothing but defeat and sorrow await you." He stared at her more intently than before. The only sound in the world was the water whispering and the nervous whinnying of her horse. At last he said, "Your mind is full of Ysbaddaden."

Medb struggled to cover her thoughts. She must think of something, someone else, but what?

It was too late. Whether by his Druid training or his ancestral feyness, Lleflys knew everything. "You haven't heard then. Ysbaddaden has given his oath to Treon."

The news dazed her. Ysbaddaden had joined her enemy? She felt a pang of such anguish it struck her immobile.

Lleflys stood on there, and not there, not much more than a dappling in the fading daylight, and then . . . he was gone.

Medb waded ashore and sat down to put on her

hose. Her pretense of ease and indifference were only protective coloration, however, and when she tried to stand, her knees failed her. She went back down. *Get up!* she told herself. But her knees gripped the earth like cedar roots.

Ysbaddaden hated her that much?

Medb, practiced in setting aside her feelings, hurried on to Moate, where she sent word to Ilbreach to either join her now or surely suffer invasion by Treon. There was another possibility: That Ilbreach would concede to Treon, who now had the great Ysbaddaden in his service. She could do nothing more than sit and wait for the outcome of events.

The hall of sickly Senchan's citadel, called Mag Brom, was a dim place with no windows, lit only by fire and a few candles. The rushes on the floor so craved freshening that Medb's heels sank a good inch into the filth. Knives and daggers had scarred the table and benches, and even when Ehtne arrived and tried to improve it, the air stank of smoke and spilled ale. The serving woman came soon after Medb's own arrival, along with Medb's councilors, Tochmarc, heavy Li Ban with Gwawl and their two children, smileless Matth, and fair-haired Fann. The household became cramped and noisy. Thankfully, Senchan himself had vacated the place, retiring to a lodge in the burgh where he could be sick in peace.

If Medb could only return to Connaught, to her

own home and the sea. The thought left her heart hungry.

But it was here, while playing chess with Daghda, that she received word that Ilbreach had taken too long to accept Medb's protection. Treon moved on him while he dallied, the Sidhe Fuait attacking before cockcrow and first light. Laois fell as easily as a hollow tree.

The events that followed moved just as Treon wanted. For him to invade Moate and challenge Medb was the only logical thing to do next. Medb sent for all her oldest and most trusted champions. One by exhausted one, they stumbled in out of the raw fog, for her call was urgent and they came as swiftly as horseflesh could carry them. Grainne, Caipre, Ainle, Bran, and Catabadh.

Medb was visited by Cowynn again. The priestess offered her peace–of a sort. "Do not refuse him this time, Lady Queen," the young Druid warned in a tone less respectful than the one she'd used in Croom.

Ehtne wordlessly offered the emissary soup, as she would any guest on so cold a day. Cowynn took it with relish. It surprised Medb to see the priestess had coarse manners at table. She talked between gulping swallows. "My king will not hesitate to declare war on you." She reached for her cup and swallowed noisily. The wine made her voice liquid as she went on. "He has a strong and aggressive nature and–" she burped, "now has Ysbaddaden as well. And Answerer, the sword given to him by Danu. He has vowed to show you no mercy."

Medb felt a swift surge of loathing. "I have fought against Ysbaddaden before. And it was I who gave him Answerer, not Danu. He will not use that sacred sword against me."

Cowynn replied with a raising of her eyebrows.

Would Ysbaddaden go so far? Medb couldn't believe it. Yet she could almost hear him say, "We must defeat Balor, by any means."

But how could he, who had been so idealistic, ally himself with Treon?

She wouldn't think of him. She must think of her people; she must go forward, despite Balor, despite Treon, despite Ysbaddaden. As she took leave of Cowynn to confer with her council, she asked them, "Should I, for our folks' sake, give in to Treon? I'm trying to think what is best for them–but I keep seeing that chill foggy night when Treon ran for his life, leaving us all to face Balor alone. I confess to you, I don't know if my desire to stand against him is rational or merely personal."

She couldn't help but wonder about Lleflys's prophecy, too. She hadn't reported her rendezvous with him to anyone, but Danu could have lost patience with her and turned instead to Treon. In which case, Medb should be glad.

She shouldn't be surprised that the wielder of Answerer, Danu's sword, had joined the ranks of the Goddess's new favorite.

"Is Ysbaddaden all that hearsay says he is?" asked Fann.

Medb nodded.

"You really did train with him? You know his skill personally?" Li Ban stepped cautiously into this questioning. By her caution, Medb realized her council had surmised, probably by her steadfast silence on the subject of her training in Ben Skellig, that it was a painful subject.

She nodded again. She'd parried his controlled attacks, and seen Skatha herself backed to the wall by him on more than one occasion. Though even with that grand swordswoman he'd used restraint. To face him in all-out combat must be a horrifying experience.

She looked from face to face down the table of Senchan's hall. These were her friends. They'd been with her since the beginning of her reign. She must tell them the truth and let them judge what was best.

"Ysbaddaden was a deadly sword arm even when I knew him. I haven't a doubt in my mind that he is now the deadliest warrior in Eire. He wields Answerer, an invincible sword granted by Danu. I cannot defeat him; none of my champions can defeat him. Not Daghda, not Arawn," she looked at Li Ban, "not even Gwawl."

The meeting fell silent, until smileless Matth said, "And yet, Ysbaddaden is not all of Treon's army. The battle to save ourselves may be fierce, but I for one don't want to call myself a Sidhe Fuait."

"Nor do I," said Tochmarc. "I will never bend my knee to Treon."

"Perhaps we should be cautious," Fann put in.

Li Ban said, "I shall not be called upon to fight, yet I think I can speak for my husband in this." She looked at Medb steadily. "He would say, 'Lead us into war, my Lady. A war without caution.' "

"Aye, I'm for war," Matth said.

Tochmarc nodded. "War."

Only Fann seemed wary, and suggested negotiation.

Medb stood and moved to the roaring fire. "Treon won't give us better terms, no matter how long we negotiate. In fact, he isn't above sending an army to attack us by surprise as we sit wishing for peace at his very table. If ever I wished for a mild solution, it's this time, but it's not possible. If we want to remain Sligo, we must fight."

When she told Cowynn her decision, the slender young Druid scoffed. "I have come to you twice now to seek your friendship and do you kindness. But you Sligo are a stubborn lot."

"Stubborn and strong. Tell your king if he wants my realm he must take it by force. He may win it or he may not, but he will certainly lose much on the day he challenges my armies."

Cowynn finished the wine in her cup, and said no when Ehtne would have refilled it. At least her drinking was moderate. "You will lose much more than my Lord by this folly."

"When faced with the rule of a lord such as Treon, I have nothing to lose."

After that, there was no choice but to hone her mind to the situation. She would not attack Treon. To stand in defense seemed the better choice. Since Treon had Ysbaddaden, as well as the benefit of greater numbers, she would make him use up at least some of his strength to get to her. Here in Moate she had the advantage of knowing the terrain, of choosing the battlefield, of setting up supply stores and deploying well-rested soldiers. Her Druids and bards assured her they could reduce the odds against her further with fire traps and tree-tangles set in the unsuspecting enemy's path.

She set guards within hailing distance of one another all along the border Treon must cross, men who were particularly keen-eyed. And then again there was nothing for her to do but wait.

The dying year and the Eve of Samhain brought its annual Fomor visit. The ogre sent to her this year was a creature so gigantic, so ugly, he was clearly meant to intimidate. "So you mean to go head-to-head with Treon, with that company of ragged knaves you call an army!" The ungainly creature gave a short harsh laugh. His name was Indech, and he came all dressed in evil. His wide snarl of a grin showed double-rows of broken teeth.

"You like to see us fight one another," said Medb.

The creature scratched his red beard, his eyes

fevered with deranged excitement. "Lord Conann and my Lord Balor aren't happy to see so much power handed to Treon as he will get when he trounces you."

"Maybe Treon won't win."

The giant broke into laughter and applause, even danced in a circle–if one could call his elephantine waddle a dance. "Treon has Ysbaddaden, who performs a thousand wondrous feats with his hallowed sword–or so they say!" He stopped dancing. "Now, if you could kill that one, both my Lords might be pleased with you. *I* might be pleased with you." His hand reached down and conspicuously rubbed his genitals.

Medb ignored the insult. "Is the Evil Eye afraid of Ysbaddaden?"

The Fomor sobered abruptly. He leaned near, and the stench of his breath assaulted her full in the face. "Lord Balor afraid? You have no idea of his true power."

She was intimidated, as she was meant to be. And in collecting Balor's tax, Indech took stores she'd depended on to use against Treon. She could only hope Balor had taken at least as much from Treon.

When she decided she could ask no one else to go against Ysbaddaden, her champions disagreed strongly. Matth spoke for them one morning in the garrison. "That is a foolish and dangerous plan, my Lady."

"It makes no matter."

"You can't take part in this battle!" Gwawl said

sharply. He sat straddling a bench.

Medb's lips fell open. He'd never spoken so bluntly to her.

"My Lady," Matth put in soothingly, "what Gwawl means is that as noble as your sacrifice might be, if you fall we all fall. There must be a better way."

She let them talk her into another plan. She didn't like their insistence on keeping her out of the fighting, however. "Even with Senchan's champions, we'll be outnumbered. We'll need every sword arm."

"We need your talent for strategy and your leadership more," Gwawl urged.

In the end, she acquiesced, knowing it was the wisest design, yet reluctant to send others into danger while she remained in the rear.

Goibhnui, Ainle, and Daghda would together seek Ysbaddaden on the field. They would capture him if they could, or wound him if they must, but kill him only as a last resort.

But what if, despite them, he still found her cowering in the rear ranks? Could he wound her, kill her? She prayed to Danu to let her champions capture him.

Snow swallowed the fields, leaving only bleached stubble above the drifts; the sky, drained of color, weighed upon the earth. The streams turned to ice and looked like dark ribbons of metal. The dark branches of Moates' forests mingled with the snow to form a lead-gray smudge along the horizon. Humankind's works looked meager compared to that ocean of cold.

Into that cold one day came a rider galloping headlong from the border shouting, "They're coming!" Inside the citadel, Medb waited with her council. Li Ban said, "Treon." Medb, by the hearth, raised her eyes from her wool carding and thought, He's here, he's come. And unlike the others, she wasn't thinking of Treon. She felt a sense of relief almost. Finally, it was time to follow this path to its ending place.

While Medb took up her place of command on a hillock behind the battlefield, the Sligo champions and their soldiers lined up for battle with faces dyed blue. The scene was a bloodcurdling cacophony of battle shrieks and blaring war trumpets embellished with bronze boars' heads. Arawn's soldiers screamed they would cut off the enemies' heads and spike them over the doors of their huts.

On the other side, Karllyl led his warriors in wild chants. They shook their thrusting spears and their bows, and praised the deeds of their fathers, and boasted of their own prowess while insulting and belittling the defenders.

When a particularly weird, discordant horn sounded, the first enemy warriors burst from their ranks and stormed forward. Immediately, the two sides surged at one another.

No sooner had they met when Treon's new cavalry of white stallions came thundering around the flanks of his infantry, threatening to crush Medb's soldiers in a pinching action. Like falcons swooping down on swallows, the horses pitched left and right, foiling any archers' aim, a dazzle of speed, manes tossing like shine off water.

The Sidhe Fuait's savagery were matched by their fighting skills and horsemanship, but if they had any weakness, it lay in Treon's strategy. Medb had taken this into account. Standing on a hillock behind the battlefield, she nodded to a man beside her, who swung up a green banner. Squadrons of four-wheeled war-chariots moved out of their hiding places in the trees, each manned by two Sligo soldiers, one driving the horses while the other hurled javelins at the enemy cavalry. The javelins were shorter than those of the Sidhe Fuait, but could be thrown with more accuracy. Their points were aimed at the enemy's white horses. A pitiable chorus of shrieks filled the air. As the animals went down, the horsemen who weren't crushed scrambled to their feet with scared faces.

When the chariots had thrown all the javelins they had, the throwers jumped out and entered the battle on the front. The drivers turned the chariots back for the woods, in case a retreat became essential.

Now Medb nodded again, and the bannerman swung a blue flag. Her own cavalry came out of their waiting places. The horsemen fought the same way as the chariots. Every mount had two riders: one threw javelins then jumped down from his horse; the other turned the animal about, tethered it into safety, and waited for the time when he was next needed. It was a new tactic she hoped would work. Mostly, battle lords simply pitted their soldiers one against the other, without keeping any in reserve. Since Treon outnumbered her to begin with, the idea had its flaw, but her intuition told her to try it.

She spotted Gwawl and the target she'd assigned him: the horned helmet of Treon. Gwawl swung his battle axe left and right, cutting down whatever man came at him. It amazed her that however soberly men made their preparations, in the midst of battle, they were transformed by the age-old blood-rage.

Ysbaddaden was harder to find, but by following the movements of Goibhnui, Ainle, and Daghda, she eventually picked him out, cutting and thrusting with his long sword, Answerer, which glowed with incandescent light as he slung it with all his skill and might.

Now Medb saw Grainne, positioned in a place of safety to one side of the battle, chanting with her runes. Soon a small cyclone came over the enemy warrior Karllyl and his soldiers, and a voracious vortex of spinning wind touched down like a howling hell hound. If Medb knew anything about Grainne's power, that unnatural wind would blow for an hour, sending blustering gales to tear through the enemy's ranks.

Caipre, too, was busy using all powers of water, earth, air, and fire at his disposal.

From her vantage, Medb saw her recent visitor, Cowyyn, busy with her own runes and magic, and soon she heard a rumbling beneath her. She was startled by something cold falling over her, down her neck, over her head, her back. She whirled to see a column of water gushing up from the ground, gyrating upward. The soldiers set to protect her tried to flee but several were swept downhill. Medb herself slithered and fell, yet managed to crawl, coughing and sputtering, against the flooding eruption to the safety of another hillock. This hillock wasn't so convenient, but now it had to do.

Chapter Eight

The battle went on. It snowed a little. Wet flakes fell on Medb's helmet and cloak. The light changed slowly in the sky above the bare winter trees as the hours passed and the numbers on both sides diminished. Fewer and then fewer soldiers occupied the field. When Karllyl was cornered against a river, he saw his efforts were in vain. He threw his sword down in the snow. His soldiers followed his lead, all throwing down their swords and lances as they were taken captive.

Treon fought on against Gwawl's forces. And Ysbaddaden, despite the three champions pitted against him, somehow managed to edge closer and closer to Medb.

Treon's woman warrior, Vivionn, screamed. She careened and fell, a spear jutting from her breast so deeply it came out at the small of her back.

The clouds parted; the sun shone through in a sudden explosion of light. Medb gave another signal, and the men who had driven the chariots and horses from the earlier attacks now took up their battle lances and blades to enter the fray. They came yelling, fresh, pent with fury, and their effect on the tiring enemy was immediate. Courage seemed to melt away from the enemy's hearts.

But then Medb cried out to see Goibhnui stagger

back, spitted on Ysbaddaden's sword. At the same time a flash-like lightning swept down on Treon's men–and held, and held. When it dissipated, at least thirteen of the invaders lay burned to death. Treon seemed to look about him in bewilderment, a suddenly wretched figure in a comical horned helmet as Gwawl's men closed in on him.

Had he not considered he might be defeated?

Medb signaled for her black horse. Mounting, she clapped her heels to the animal's sides and rode toward Treon through the churned snow of the battlefield. Dead lay men everywhere, their dead eyes reflecting the afternoon sky as she galloped past. Soon the vultures would turn on their wide wings above this place.

She reigned her horse suddenly where Treon stood surrounded by threatening Sligo. She shouted, "Do you yield?"

He grimaced, and she thought he would do something stupid, something desperate and proud and reckless. But then his fingers loosened their grip on his sword and it slipped into the snow. Gwawl lunged forward to take him prisoner. Medb felt no triumph, but only wheeled her horse for the corner of the field where Ysbaddaden's burning sword cast lights and shadows wildly across the snow. As he fought on against Daghda and Ainle, the latter's weapon twisted from his hand and went flying. Skatha's old trick, the same one Medb had used on Arawn. Ysbaddaden turned all his attention to

Daghda. A timely sweep wounded the man's knee and sent him sprawling, crying out in pain. Ysbaddaden swung about to find Ainle with his back against a tree, holding a broken spear he'd found on the ground. Its shaft was shorter than Ysbaddaden's sword, making it useless, in fact, dangerous.

Medb's horse seemed to run like a horse in a nightmare, not fast enough, in slow-motion. As she rode through the remnants of the battle, she had time to look at Ainle. His face was white, but his eyes were terribly dark, fixed on Ysbaddaden's sword.

The nightmare fell away; Medb's horse sped. She drove its shoulder into Ysbaddaden's left shoulder, and jumped off even as the animal raced on. As if he hadn't noticed he'd been hit by a horse, Ysbaddaden righted his balance and his attention on Ainle. Medb picked herself up out of the snow and raced to catch his sword arm. His head whipped down as she cried his name. "Ysbaddaden!" Their eyes met.

"It's over!" she shouted.

He hardly seemed to recognize her. Looking at him, she was terrified. He was smiling, not with savagery, but with joy. There was a light, a glory, in his face that shouldn't be discovered on any human face. She knew men went mad in battle; there were berserkers who foamed at the mouth and raged like dogs, but Ysbaddaden wasn't a berserker.

Yet with that total foreignness in his eyes she knew he could kill her where she stood and not even notice that it was her.

The arm in her grip didn't shake her off, however. "Ysbaddaden, Treon has surrendered!"

Slowly the glory faded from his gaze. The smile fell from his lips. His arm relaxed, and she dared to release her hold. She stood away from him, and saw the light go from his sword. That symbol of Danu's mystery became a mere piece of edged iron, cold in the winter sun. He lowered it until its point dug into the churned snow. He leaned on its jewel-crested hilt wearily, heaving to catch his breath.

Ainle, still holding the broken spear as his last defense, now threw the weapon aside. His back slid down the tree trunk, and he flung himself on his face, almost sobbing in relief.

Medb looked around and saw that Daghda sat holding his wounded knee. He flicked Ysbaddaden a fierce look.

Otherwise, there were only corpses sprawled in the snow. One of them was Goibhnui.

Medb looked again at Ysbaddaden, and felt as if she'd just opened her eyes to see a being from a song she had loved in childhood.

His eyes, however, filled with barbs as he panted, "Great Queen . . . I suppose I am your prisoner, a poor wretch, and helpless . . . and you, descendant of dead and departed sovereigns, you are Queen-to-be of all Eire . . . whether or not either of us wishes it anymore."

* * *

Medb's long skirts trailed down steps cut from solid rock as she followed two guards beneath the citadel of Mag Brom. Knowing she couldn't rest until the confrontation with Treon was over, she'd elected to hold it tonight. She'd washed, changed, and eaten since the battle, and now it was late. Nonetheless, she'd see her prisoner and put a finish to her long hatred.

He'd been placed in a cell away from that shared by Ysbaddaden and the other surviving Sidhe Fuait champions. Along the grim passage, Medb's guards turned a sudden corner, then descended a few more dark steps finally to fling back a door.

The tiny cell wasn't lit. Medb carried her own candle inside. The only other light came from outside the open door, where the two guards, with another candle between them, hovered protectively, out of sight but not out of earshot. Treon sat on the dank stone floor, his knees drawn up, his back against the far corner. Medb had given orders for him to be shackled hand and foot, more to impress him with his situation than to prevent his escape, which was impossible at any rate.

"My Lord King Treon," she said, but not with any great ceremony.

He blinked at her owlishly, adjusting to the light she'd brought into his dark solitude. "Not anyone's lord at the moment," he muttered.

"Nor ever again."

He didn't show any emotion, only stared at the

flame of her candle.

"Twice you have done me grievous harm. Once today and once the night you bargained with Conann for your life, leaving my family to fight the Evil Eye alone–and to die."

His voice held all his weariness. "But *you* didn't die, did you? More's the pity."

Medb controlled her temper with effort. "I'm not surprised you feel that way now."

His gaze sharpened. "Did you come here to taunt me? It doesn't become a queen. One thing you never learned, Medb, was the use of power. Just tell me what you want. My oath of allegiance? Very well, you have it."

She made no secret of her disgust. "You have sworn such vows before. Not a dog under the table believes you anymore. No, your hour is done. You are exiled from this land."

He jerked, though he must have known she would do this.

"You may go wherever you wish, as far as the wind blows and the rain falls, as far as the sun revolves, the sea circles and the earth extends–but never here, never again."

After a moment, he said, "Ysbaddaden didn't think you had the iron to challenge Balor. He might be wrong." He almost smiled. "Or maybe now that you're getting your revenge–"

"If I were merely seeking revenge, I wouldn't exile you. I would tether you to a post and let loose starving dogs on you from all sides. For I hate you with a heart and a half, Treon."

She took a step back, then turned for the door of the cell. Without looking at him again, she said, "At first light, you'll be escorted to the coast. There, you'll be given your cloak, sword, shield, dagger, and a boat with enough supplies aboard to keep you alive for a week. If you haven't found a safe haven by then . . . more's the pity."

The guards closed the door on him, and Medb had started up the stairs when she heard him cry, "You dishonor yourself and all the Sligo tribe with this sentence!"

Rain drummed on the world outside smoky, windowless Mag Brom the next day. Treon had been taken away hours earlier, and Medb, dressed in a skirt and bodice of saffron cloth, interviewed the defeated Sidhe Fuait champions one by one, beginning with Cowynn.

The young Druid knelt before Medb's high seat and offered her oath before she was asked. "I had no idea how base Treon's ambitions were, my Lady. He shockingly betrayed my trust. If you will give me a second chance, I pledge you my service and companionship."

Medb studied her comely, soft face. Would she betray the Sligo? "I will accept your oath of service, Cowynn, but I don't want your companionship. I'll send you to Aran Isle, my most remote province. If you are wise, you will serve me there diligently and without flash and noise."

The creature bent her rough, silver head and kissed Medb's hand so hard it smarted.

The bards, dark Darvyd and balding Cymri, accepted her terms reluctantly. But the warrior Karllyl flatly refused. "My father served Treon's father, and my grandfather served his grandfather. I'm sworn to Treon till the day I die."

"Treon is gone, and will never return."

"Then exile me with him."

She liked his staunch loyalty better than Cowynn's pretensions of remorse, the same as she'd rather put her trust in a stubborn river than the veer of a gull. "I can't exile you for the crime of remaining true to your lord, nor can I give Treon a companion to encourage false hopes of rebuilding an army." Medb folded her hands in her lap. "I wish you would reconsider, my Lord," she said gently. "I could use a man of your skills."

He wouldn't move from his position, however.

"The only thing I can do then is release you, with great sorrow, for the life of a wanderer is harsh. Your arms will of course be restored to you at the border of Sligo lands. You'll always find welcome in my hospitality tents or in my legions."

Softened, he bowed gravely. "My Lady." Yet with that he took his leave of Moate.

Only Ysbaddaden's fate remained to be decided.

Whereas the others had been uneasy, like house

cats in a strange room, the great swordsman seemed utterly relaxed. Even without his armor and weapon he appeared dangerous. It was ten years since he and Medb had parted. She'd been sixteen winters then, and he not above eighteen. He lifted his brows as he stood before her now, a hint of the old mockery touching his lips.

"I understand why you joined Treon against me," she said without prelude. "I can see how you might mistakenly mesh your private obsession with his greed to create in your mind a shared purpose. But Treon's reckless ambition was never your own."

"At least Treon *had* an ambition."

"He had a scheme. He used you, and you let him. I was surprised to hear it, since I'd assumed you'd learned better from your experiences. I've followed your doings, and watched you serve one petty tyrant after another, and one after another leave them, embittered."

He leaned forward enough to say quietly, "Since you taught me all there is to know of bitterness, Princess, the lessons learned from others came as no wonder."

Princess. She must hold herself above the reaction she felt. He must give her the respect she had earned. "You must call me Queen now. I have worn that title for many a year."

He smiled. A not quite harmless smile, like sunshine on mountain crags. "May the due honor be yours, my Lady Queen. *I* am not the one to withhold it. That is for Balor to do."

Annoyed at his completely unvanquished bearing, she said shortly, "Do you agree to join the Sligo? Or will you go your own way as always, seeking a ruler who doesn't exist?"

His brown eyes glowed. "As you say, the ruler I seek doesn't exist, but these folk gathered around you will have dire need of my sword before long. The Evil Eye sees you full now, Medb. You can't hide from him any longer, not after the display of battle tactics you showed yesterday. And when he comes for you . . . well, *someone* must greet him with the blade-edge he deserves."

The thought came clear and cold and hard in her mind: Does he think I'm not capable of defending my people without him?

"I'll join your tribe," he went on, "but only if you swear to not send me to a distant court as you will Cowynn. And don't try to use me to undertake wars of acquisition for you. I've had enough of that. I must be at your side, day and night, because, unless you make a muddle of it after all, you're going to wear the crown promised you by prophecy, and soon now. When that happens, Conann and the Evil Eye will both be hard on your heels."

Medb hadn't looked beyond defeating Treon, but she knew that by doing so she had become the most powerful force in Eire by default. How had this happened when she'd never sought it, never wanted it? Apparently Lleflys had been wrong; Danu hadn't changed Her mind.

Without arguing, she rose, signaling the interview was over. "I agree to your terms. Consider yourself one of my personal guardsmen. And now, if you'll excuse me, I must visit the wounded."

"I'll accompany you. I must make amends to some of them if I'm to become a comrade-in-arms."

It was Daghda he meant, foremost. In the garrison, Grainne was doing her best to relieve the champion's pain. As the beauty she seemed so unaware of hit Medb's eyes, the bard said, "The scoundrel is grumbling, but he'll not lose the leg."

Through gritted teeth, Daghda said to Ysbaddaden, "Your hard iron pains me worse than the bite of a horse-leech! I damn the fire wherein your sword was shaped!"

"Damn me, not Answerer, which was forged by the Goddess."

Daghda shook his head. "I'll not damn the man who may be fighting at my back soon."

Medb doubted Daghda would ever fight again, but the tragedy of that hardly struck her during this exchange, for Ysbaddaden's words still rang in her mind: The Evil Eye sees you, Medb. You can't hide from him any longer. She prayed silently, *Danu, I would be content to stay quiet and labor on for my people, but You have proven that Your will is greater than mine. Therefore I trust You to lead my footsteps to whatever end You have ordained for me.*

* * *

Ysbaddaden treated his queen with unfailing courtesy. Rather too much courtesy. As he predicted, Balor seemed incensed by Medb's victory over Treon. As the season of Samhain relinquished its grip of snow and ice, allowing green Imbolc to return, reports of Fomor raids came to her from every province. She felt as though she'd stepped into the grip of forces she couldn't understand, and certainly couldn't defy.

At the same time, not all of Treon's provinces were willing to accept her as their ruler. She had to journey to each individually, to negotiate peace or quell hostility. She bade Senchan farewell, and wished him better health, while she set out for Kilcullen. Bringing it under her banner would isolate Athy, making that province in turn more likely to grant her an alliance. Her council accompanied her, as did Gwawl, who wouldn't leave his pregnant wife just now. And Ysbaddaden, who had appointed himself her shadow. Fann suggested she ought to feel protected, but Medb didn't feel protected. She felt confined; he was her jailer of a new sentence of isolation.

Just over the border of Kilcullen, Li Ban, who hadn't expected her child for several more weeks, admitted she was feeling the pangs of birth. The company made camp at a place called Bliancarrig. The slender rock for which the place was named was a rude but impressive monument; its shape indicated that it must have played a role in ancient fertility rites.

Gwawl had equipped a cart for Li Ban, a sturdy vehicle drawn by two oxen, covered with tent-cloth. Inside, in the early evening, she gave birth to their third child.

Medb was sitting beside the open fire when the newborn made its first cry. She exchanged a smile with Matth and Tochmarc. Fann was in the cart with the new parents. Soon Gwawl came out smiling in his bashful way, his face lit with wonder. "A boy," he said, "small but healthy. And Li Ban does well."

Medb felt a rush of love for both warrior and scribe. She rose to clasp his shoulders. "Congratulations."

Ysbaddaden, sitting across the fire, watched this without expression. But when everyone else had hailed Gwawl's good fortune, he made a visible effort. "You're a lucky man, Gwawl." Medb caught herself wondering if he'd ever missed not having a wife and children, if he had any regrets about the choices he'd made–or she'd made.

The child safely delivered, the night's guards were chosen from among the soldiers accompanying them, and soon the company sought their tents. The encampment grew still.

A pendant sparked in the mat of dark bristles on the Fomor's chest, and more stolen gold winked on his short, hairy fingers. His companions were all equally well jeweled. A week ago, they'd raided a holding in Kilcullen, burning the houses to the ground, driving off the cattle, and scattering the stores of grain. They'd fed well on the spoils of that assault, but they hadn't eaten in the two days since. For Fomors, feasting was a passion second only to warfare, and they grumbled to Indech, their leader.

Indech wasn't a creature of vast intelligence, though he owned slightly more than his three subordinates, who were of that lower order of Fomor, more animal than sentient being, without benefit of human blood in their veins. He'd smelled something promising earlier this evening, and had led his minions along the faint trail of scent. One of his underlings had muttered a comment about his leadership that had earned the brute a thump from Indech's club. They followed along silently now.

They traveled in the dark, not needing sleep, sleep not being one of the Fomor's natural rhythms. Finally Indech saw a light, little points of brightness piercing the black forest, and all through his body he felt a thrumming of eagerness. A camp of humans. And that scent–unmistakably it was newborn baby, tender and delicate-fleshed. His mouth watered.

He found the camp well guarded, but that was hardly a problem for brutes who towered a foot or more over the largest human male. Indech made a circle around the edge of darkness beyond the central fire, to judge how many and where the sentries were set.

Four. No problem. He gave each Fomor, including himself, a sentry to attack. When he made the sound of an owl, they rushed the humans, breaking their necks and bashing their heads. Indech took his from behind, snapping the man's neck with a jerk. All without a single sound of warning.

If he had been less hungry, he might have been more cautious, might have hung back in the darkness to see exactly who occupied the tents. But his belly's needs–and that tantalizing scent of newborn flesh–made him daring. At any rate, he wasn't accustomed to being refused, and his digestive juices had already begun to flow in anticipation. He and his minions moved directly toward the lighted cart, intent on the baby.

A guttering lamp lit the inside of the cart. Gwawl had thanked Fann and sent her to bed. He alone watched over his wife and son. Li Ban slept. Their other children were in one of the tents, with their nurse-woman. Gwawl touched the blunt, callused tip of his finger to his youngest child's cheek. The boy looked like Li Ban. His heart felt full to overflowing, but, never very articulate, he merely whispered, "Danu, thank you for Your blessings."

As he stretched his shoulders, a frisson passed up his spine. Almost as the same instant, the cart jolted, yawning to one side, as if some great ox were trying to overturn it. Knocked off his knees, Gwawl grabbed for a handhold to keep from landing on Li Ban and the baby.

Her eyes blinked wide open. "What was that!"

Before he could reply, the cart jolted once more, and careened to the left. Then its wheels started to roll. Gwawl leaned forward and opened the front curtains, straining to see past the light cast by the lamp. He saw two huge Fomor in tandem pulling the tongue of the cart out of the camp. It shuddered and rolled from side to side as it picked up speed.

Where were his sentries? Frustrated rage seized Gwawl as he fumbled for his battle axe. Li Ban, her face an ashy white, gathered her child closer and screamed, "Help us!" The cartwheels bounced over a root, and Gwawl fell on top of her, smothering her further cries. The lamp went out. Gwawl felt a sharp spark of rage behind his eyes.

Whenever Medb slept, part of her mind always stood watch. Tonight it was on duty as usual. She stirred in her blankets, then woke without knowing what roused her. She lay listening and feeling. Suddenly she heard a muffled cry for help and a rumble of cartwheels. At the same time she whiffed the stinging stench of Fomors.

Another sound, this time a squeal, startled her to her feet. Sword and shield in hand, fairly humming with energy, she ran from her tent to find Li Ban's cart gone. She peered into the dark beyond the lowering firelight to see the cart pitching through the trees. But someone was between it and her. Ysbaddaden stood over a fallen Fomor, the source of the squeal Medb had heard.

Another creature, wild-haired and wearing nothing but animal skins, came at Ysbaddaden from behind. "Turn!" Medb shouted. He reacted, and threw up his luminous blade to block the creature's massive club.

Medb ran to help him as Gwawl tumbled out the back of the cart, his axe in one hand, Li Ban in his free arm, their baby in her embrace. He fell to his knees with this burden. "The baby!" Medb cried. "The stinking brutes are after the baby!" As she ran toward the new parents, Gwawl shouted, "Two more of them are pulling the cart!"

But the Fomors, feeling their load escape them, left off pulling and now appeared at either side of the back of the cart. Gwawl came to his feet swinging his weapon, putting himself between the creatures and his wife, who huddled in her nightdress, her whole body curved protectively around the bundle in her arms.

Medb leapt to block the leader of the pack, a huge specimen himself, though dressed in clothing instead of skins, and more human-like in his features. Nonetheless, he made sounds like a grunting pig. Sweat poured from him, as if even for him the huge axe in his right hand was too much. She blocked the first blow of his weapon, but as the axe came right back, she dodged to the side, stumbled, and struggled to recover her footing.

The creature spoke between piggish grunts. "You

puny islanders are no match for Fomor strength. Give us the baby and we'll let you live."

She recognized that voice: Indech. She didn't answer him, for she was too busy blocking his blows. He was twice as strong as she, however, and she knew he was going to kill her. She fought on simply because there was nothing else to do. And because something inside her refused to surrender Li Ban's baby.

Don't think about it. Just *do* it.

Indech's axe swung, caught her magical shield squarely, and though the metal held, she was sent sprawling onto her back. She looked up at the predator's eyes. But before he could finish her, Ysbaddaden challenged him with a minatory growl. "Here, you rank piece of filth!"

The Fomor paused, only for the space of a single heartbeat, then, with a grunt of expelled stench, he forgot Medb and lunged at Ysbaddaden.

As the swordsman parried the swing of that deadly battle axe, Medb took a double-handed hold of her sword and swung it with all her strength, a back-handed stroke that made contact with the Fomor's axe-wielding arm. His grunting rose to a shrill screech as his right arm was hewed to the bone above the elbow.

Another sound burst from the beast fighting Gwawl, a din of rage and pain, but Medb didn't dare look away from Indech to see what it meant.

Indech's wound poured greenish blood. As he

stumbled back, Ysbaddaden's sword lunged. The Fomor sucked in his gut to avoid the blade, then turned and ran.

Medb turned to see Gwawl's foe fall and lay still, his mouth gaping to show a lower jaw studded with pin-prick teeth. Gwawl staggered back. He had five ragged scratch marks down his ruddy cheek. But Medb saw something she'd never seen before: three Fomor brutes lay dead. It was unthinkable, but they'd won.

Slowly, the torn edges of the world closed together again. Gwawl gathered his kneeling wife in his arms. "They're dead, you're safe, you're safe."

Li Ban wept softly and clung to him with one arm, her baby cradled in the other. "Are you all right?" she sobbed. "Oh, look what they've done to you." She petted his scratched face.

Medb felt left out of that scene, so intimate and emotional. Ysbaddaden stood near her, his raspy breath coming in bursts as he too watched the loving couple. As his battle fire abated, he turned to Medb and said, "You fought well."

She nodded. "And you."

He bowed; it was like a tree's great, slow gesture in a wind.

She realized she'd come out in her nightdress. She rubbed the tops of her bare arms.

He gestured to the dead brutes and grinned suddenly. "The Evil Eye's ham-fisted domination is growing feeble. Can you feel it?"

"I don't know." She looked at the fallen Fomors.

She'd never seen even one of them bested before. She felt stunned and stupid by the realization that they could be killed. "I don't know what anything means anymore. I can't take it in somehow. I think maybe I'm just . . . past this. I'm too battered."

"Don't be silly," Ysbaddaden said with disgust.

It was hardly an exchange on par with that between Gwawl and Li Ban. Ysbaddaden turned away to bend over one of the stinking corpses. When he stood again, he wore an expression she'd never seen before. "Look at this." He held a pendant with a precious stone that gave a soft clear radiance. As Medb took it, it began to sparkle. "What is it?"

"It's the Stone of Might," Li Ban said as Gwawl helped her to her feet.

Medb held the pendant toward the failing firelight. She remembered stories about a stone of indescribable antiquity called the Stone of Might. Supposedly it endowed its wearer with formidable strength. It lay in a superb enamel and jewel-work setting.

"Why didn't it help *him?*" Ysbaddaden gestured at the dead Fomor.

"The power is given by Danu," Li Ban said.

Medb turned to Gwawl, and pressed the stone into his hands. "It's yours."

"No . . . I'm not worthy. You should wear it yourself. Or Ysbaddaden."

"I have my shield, and Ysbaddaden has his Answerer. Danu seems to want my finest champions strengthened by her gifts."

Gwawl turned the trophy in his hands, studying its every angle in absorbed doubt. "Never in my wildest fantasies did I imagine I would one day hold the Stone of Might."

Medb understood, even as her agile mind was having trouble taking it all in.

It was Li Ban who finally took the pendant from Gwawl and slung the cord over his head, so that the glinting stone fell onto his chest. After a moment, she tucked it inside his tunic where it didn't show. Then she patted his chest in wifely satisfaction.

Medb couldn't say that he looked different, yet something *was* different about him. She hoped she hadn't cursed him with a strength that would only call misfortune down on his head.

A breeze like a stiff broom brushed Medb as she stood in her saffron gown and embroidered cloak in the center of the glade. The broad gold and bronze leaves over her head danced, and above them a cackling of geese winged southward.

How had she come to stand here, in this most sacred place in Eire, beneath this great oak, before this gathering of rulers, Druids, bards, and warriors?

She'd had little rest; it had been a nervous night, with sleep a skin that never altogether formed over her anxious thoughts. Ehtne had dressed her before it was light, and a procession had conducted her here at the very moment of the chrome-yellow moon's setting. The great diviner Adna led the march, brandishing his carved Poet's Rod, with the image of a bird on the tip of it, the symbol of his power as the supreme bard in Eire. He was six foot five in height, with grizzled hair with red flecks, a concise, full beard, and blue eyes with heavy brows. Behind him came lesser bards with harps, all dressed alike, in beautiful flowing draperies of snowy cloth. The frozen grass crunched under their footsteps.

Then came Ceridwen, recently elected Archdruid of Eire by her fellow divines. Then Medb, then the other Druids, so many of them, all in robes of most exquisite loveliness.

Medb felt the power of the site the instant she'd entered it. It riveted her with awe. The Grand Oak and its companion trees were the oldest and largest in Eire. She sensed that humankind was nothing compared to them. Through their roots, they fed on the Earth, while their raised arms supported the sky.

That was how she'd arrived at this *place*, but how had she come to this *position*, which she'd never wanted? She closed her eyes to look back at the landscape of the past parading inside her closed lids: Had it started when she'd gone to war against Nuada to protect her folk in Ahascragh? Or when she revealed her sword skill to recruit Arawn and Goibhnui? Or was it the moment she picked up her dead brother's sword in rage against Conann?

By the time she'd pitted herself against Treon in

Moate, it had been too late to recall her course. In the five months since, she'd conquered or calmed all the wrangling and discontent in Treon's previous holdings and in four new provinces; she'd fought two more wars.

In retrospect, it seemed as though she'd had no choice but to gain this position among the federation of neighboring peoples called the Tuatha de Dannan.

As the light brightened toward daybreak, the Druid's footsteps stirred up the tea-like tang of moldering leaves as they began a sunwise circling of the Grand Oak. The chanters also began their work.

Their voices filled the grove, calling on the hallowed names of the sun and the winds and the waters while their feet wove a complex design on the earth. The bards beyond murmured in counterpoint to the Druid's chanting. Adna gestured with his magical ash rod. The limpid autumn morning dimmed, the air chilled, grew dense, thick with tension. The chanting rose to a thunder. Then, as the first rays of the sun struck the uppermost branches of the great tree, Ceridwen lifted her arms. The Druids halted in midstep, freezing the pattern. Like naked twigs, Ceridwen's fingers tore the space above her head. The sound was rent from the grove, hurled into the sky–and then it was gone.

Chapter Nine

Ceridwen's calm face in the aftermath wore a gentle expression. Her eyelids were lightly closed, her lips softly moving in silent adoration. The Druids again began to circle and chant, this time a familiar song for the oaks. The ritual swirled on around Medb like a mist. She tried to concentrate on the tree at her back, the Grand Oak of Eire, whose huge arms cast shadows over the assembly beyond the priests, priestesses, and bards.

Not everyone had come, of course, but eleven provinces had sent representatives to honor and acclaim her. No less than two hundred spectators watched in fascinated silence.

There was no denying the powerful spiritual presence of this secret sacred site, which even Balor knew nothing about. Many of the majestic trees were of immense age, judging by their firth and height. Danu had revealed the site as sacred so many generations ago that no one remembered the circumstances, but the Druids who guarded its approaches would give their lives rather than let any foreigner desecrate it. No common clamor was allowed to disturb the sacred atmosphere, and so closely kept was its secret that there was no fear of any disruption of this holiest and most impressive of all ceremonies.

The Druid song for the oaks tightened into another rhythmic chant that stopped when Ceridwen spread her arms wide; with sprigs of sacred mistletoe in both hands, she began to speak with beautiful solemnity. "By the laws that govern our natural world, and by the supreme power vested in me as Archdruid, we name you, Medb, High Ruler of Eire. Magnified and sanctified be your name."

Another Druid stepped forward to hand Ceridwen a purple velvet pillow with an object covered with a white cloth. The bearer of this should have been Lleflys, acknowledged as the second most powerful priest in the land, but he had failed to appear. Therefore, Gwydion, the third-ranking priest, held the honor.

Ceridwen uncovered the pillow to reveal the glowing, round Lia Fail. It caused a murmur of awe among the assembly. Medb too had murmured when she'd found the round talisman, about the size of her fist, in her chamber one morning after she had dreamed of Danu. As she took it from Ceridwen now, she looked down into its jeweled clarity and wondered what would come next. Each mote of sunlight became a mote of separate brilliance within it, yet it revealed no secrets such as she wished to see. Neither had the Goddess spoken to her in her dream to give her guidance, though Her face had expressed kindness and serenity, as if She simply trusted Medb to know what to do.

Ceridwen gave a signal that the ceremony was over, and the people surged forward to engulf Medb in acclamation and praise. None of them seemed to notice how frightened she was, how deeply she hated this fate she had tried so hard to elude. In retrospect, she saw that every evasion had only brought it closer. Those whom the gods choose have nowhere to hide.

She concentrated on the faces before her. Some she knew well: Tochmarc, wearing a fierce, protective scowl; loyal, boyish Ainle; flame-headed Daghda; beautiful Grainne; Caipre with his oaken harp; Catabadh, so sly for a Druid; handsome Cowynn, even slyer; silver-bearded Diancecht the Healer; earnest Gwawl. Some she had formed attachments to only recently: Curoi, former ruler of treacherous Tir Tairn, now her ally; craggy-faced Llugh, the warrior-king from Tara; a large, wild-looking woman called Nemhain of the Dyfedh tribe.

Only when the crowd began to shout and laugh and gesticulate among themselves, forgetting her a little, did Ysbaddaden offer his formal words of respect. "The jewel in your hands dispenses light over us all, my Lady High Ruler." The morning sun accentuated the chiseled planes of his face, a full head above hers.

"Does it?" Her tongue wanted to let loose words she knew she mustn't say: Why did Danu reunite us when it's obviously too late for us to be friends anymore, when I am finally resigned to my death?

She knew that wasn't fair. Her death was hardly so important as the freedom of Eire. She wasn't thinking clearly. She felt irritable, resentful, disconnected, all at the same time. Her eyes flicked to the throng come to honor her. Didn't they know she couldn't do what they wanted? They thought that now, because they'd named her High Ruler, she could lead them into battle with a shout and a trumpet and drive Balor out of the land. That was the cornerstone of the legend they were building about her. But it was impossible. They looked to her to lead them, and she would if they insisted–into havoc and annihilation. The lists of the dead would stretch from corner to corner of Eire.

Ceridwen's peaceful features appeared at Her side again. "Remember, the Goddess has us all in her hand." And by that Medb knew the priestess had heard her unstated words.

"You are naturally of two minds today, my Lady. And that is good. The Mysteries only unfold to a mind in flux, facing two ways at once."

"Then mine is in the perfect condition. May Danu bless it with some plan."

"She will, you'll see. Danu will provide everything you need when the time comes."

"And when will that be?"

Ceridwen shrugged. "Who can say except you?"

Long narrow trestle tables stood beneath huge copper oaks outside the sacred grove. Serving folk had decorated the tables with shiny loaves of braided bread and bunches of syringa and a few late purple orchids which flourished wild in the woods. To partake of the feast, all the champions and rulers settled in their places on the long benches, according to their rank and precedence. The common folk lounged on spread cloaks in the sun, while Medb sat in a chair provided for her at the head table. As they ate, Darvyd sang so sweetly he charmed the assembly into losing track of the time.

Then Adna told a tale featuring certain beautiful virgins of the Otherworld. Ceridwen shed her aura of dark prophetic powers to chide him: "The heroic men in these tales are always rewarded with the love and the pleasure of beautiful dream-women. But what are heroic women rewarded with? Husbands! And quicker than sneezes, children, too! Where is the justice?"

As laughter passed along the tables, Medb noticed the perimeter of guards stop several oncoming riders. Fair-haired Finola, entrusted with protecting the celebrants, whipped off her bench with all the purpose of a veteran warrior. Her soldiers surrounded the late arrivals; Medb heard a strained voice call out, "What do I have to do to see this High Ruler you've elected?"

The men were allowed to come before Medb; Nuada the Silver-handed, whom she had deposed and disgraced years ago, led them. He looked a little older, a little rougher, and much dirtier, and she comprehended at once that he had changed a great deal. He reluctantly went to one knee before her.

"Please, my Lord, rise up, and tell me what brings you in such a lather."

"Conann," he panted, "has destroyed Omagh."

Matth's red head jerked up. "What do you mean?"

"He's destroyed it! There's no other word I can use!" Nuada's voice was savage. "He's turned it into a wasteland! There's nothing left! *Nothing!*"

What he said didn't affected Medb so much as the chilling sound of this fierce man's voice breaking. Tears of anger and hate and disbelief filled his eyes. "There are no folk left, not a tree still stands . . . " He gestured helplessly to the oaks under which they celebrated. "The streams run with foul water. He leveled everything to the ground, and his beasts butchered with hideous savagery. Even unfortified burghs were burned down, and the women, the old folk, the children slaughtered! Or put to flight. There's naught but a rock-strewn plain filled with corpses. My own men fought to the last. I had a regiment, and only these few with me came out of the fray. One of the beasts even wrenched my sword out of my very grip." Overcome, he lowered his white face into his hands.

Gasps came from up and down the tables. Warriors rose, their hands searching their belts for the weapons put aside for this day of peace. Medb struggled to take it in: beautiful Omagh nothing but a flat plane of rocks? All those hard-working, merry folk dead? How could that be?

Everyone talked and shouted at once, until reliable Gwawl stood on his bench and shouted, "Silence! Let the High Ruler speak!"

The High Ruler. Medb realized that meant her. She didn't know what they expected her to say. As each pair of eyes grounded on her, however, the indignity of this latest outrage embedded itself in her very heart and core. And there the deepest stubborn stronghold opened itself, and loosed its grasp.

"Enough," she said softly, "we've had enough." She looked up and down the tables at the many faces watching hers. She paused for an instant to look at Gwawl's second child, clutching Li Ban's skirts apprehensively.

"Go now, all of you." She made a gesture of dismissal. "Go out from here and tell each person you meet, every man and woman with a weapon, or with runes and the knowledge to use them, that Eire has had enough. Enough death, enough fear, enough theft and felony, enough violation to last her from now until time itself ends. 'Fomor rule will last forever?' How often have we heard that?"

Her fists lifted to either side of her head in sudden emphasis. "*I say it shall not!* It is *finished!* Balor shall hold our hearts in dread no more. Send word to every man, woman, and child that henceforth the Tuatha de Danann are a *free people!* The fear and destruction are at their end!"

Her voice quivered with emotion she looked from one face to another. "Go from this place and spread the news. And tell all who would fight for liberty to meet me at the borders of Omagh."

"Free!" Darvyd's rich voice shouted, "Free!"

It grew into a chant of voices that filled the glorious bronze autumn woods and soared toward the skies above.

For a second, Medb's thoughts returned to Connaught, to the wide purity of the westering sea. She shook her head in sorrow, knowing she would never see it again. She would lose all in this battle, and she accepted the knowledge finally and fatefully, as a condemned woman might accept a bowl of poison. Danu had given her the Lia Fail, and through it she had made a pact with her people that she was bound to keep.

But when had it all started? She would never unweave that fabric now. She saw that sometimes the great changes, the ones that cleave time, happen so deep and silent that one can't know when they occurred.

In the clamor of leave-taking, she saw Ysbaddaden. He stood grinning back at her in savage satisfaction. She looked away only to catch the eye of Ceridwen, who seemed to smile slightly and nod, as if to say, You see; Danu provides.

Aye, Danu provides, Medb thought. And Danu takes away.

* * *

Ride to war! Balor has attacked Omagh!

Medb sent out her call and Eire heard it. Patriots began to gather in Strabane, a raw, windy place near the border of Omagh. Dependable men came in brightly colored tunics, glittering with edged, long-bladed thrusting spears, and gleaming, short throwing spears in quivers, and blades in sheathes flashing at their hips. The shields flung behind their shoulders were painted in rich colors. Kings and their finest warriors came wearing mail, shining like salmon scales. Lesser men came in leather vests sewn with metal. Even those few obdurate rulers and champions who had scorned naming Medb High Ruler came now and gave her their pledges.

Sinnan Og of the Falias tribe came on a bright day with six hounds, great gray beasts whose collars shone with silver. Calatin, of the Bri Leith, arrived with a hawk on his shoulder ruffling its sharp-edged feathers and brilliant, glaring, avian eyes. "When I heard your summons," he told Medb, "it was as though my mind cleared at last. I realized I had been beguiled by the spell of the Evil Eye." He had a voice as dry and ponderous as creaking timbers. "Balor fostered distrust and kept us all bickering with each other so we wouldn't combine against him."

Sinnan Og agreed. "He came from out of the primeval dark when the world was first formed." She turned her head to spit in contempt. "And now we'll send him back there."

Even Lleflys came, one cold moonlit night. He accosted Medb outside her tent in his fey there-there manner, and said, with a stiff smile pasted on his lips, "I see you've gathered all the tribes to your rule. Yet your power is no match for that of the Otherworld."

She had no time for his ambiguity. Instead, she reminded him that he'd been wrong about her before. "Tell me you've foreseen my defeat, then, so I can take hope of winning."

It was a time for heroes, and it wasn't long until she had a pantheon of them. As the weather grew cooler, they encamped around her. Men from her own tribe served as her escort whenever she went among them, and Ysbaddaden remained always at her side. All told, there were almost fifty warriors, well trained and with the seasoning of the years behind them, and again as many spellcasters with their runes. By day, the soldiers they each commanded practiced with their weapons, while the mages consulted and worked minor charms to enhance the army's strength and ability. The sight of that great host stirred something in Medb, and she too spent as much time as she could to improve herself in the arts of war.

She was throwing spears at a straw mark one day when she heard a voice, familiar yet forgotten: "You are better with a sword, my Lady High Ruler."

Medb turned and shaded her eyes against the sun. A female figure dipped gracefully to one knee.

"I offer you my skill and my heart in this endeavor."

"Skatha?" She stepped forward to raise the swordswoman up. "You've come, too?"

Skatha stood back, her hand resting on the gold hilt of her sword. Medb saw the glint of chain mail beneath her woolen over-tunic. Skatha smiled, and light touched her eyes. "What choice did I have when I heard that the High Ruler had proclaimed Eire free? 'Meet me on the borders of Omagh!' the messengers quoted. So," she made a shrugging gesture, "here I am."

"Here we all are," Ysbaddaden said, stepping forward to greet his old instructor.

"Ah, now, this is like old times." The swordswoman clasped his arm.

"Better than old times."

"You think so? Then you haven't changed, have you? As for me," she looked around at the encampment, "I can feel the Evil Eye on us, I can feel his anger and violence coming."

"We don't expect to meet him in Omagh," Medb said. "We think he'll send Conann."

"Don't be surprised if you get more than you anticipate. Balor is capable of ambush. He'll do everything he can to bring us ruin and turn our hopes to despair once more. He would laugh to steal our victory and leave us mourning our dead."

To Ysbaddaden, she said, "You still have the sword Medb gave you?"

He drew Answerer half out of its sheath. The

blade gleamed with unnatural brightness in the sunlight.

Skatha nodded. "You'll have need of it. We can be sure the Evil Eye and his supernatural demons are inventing deep cunning thoughts of their own."

Ceridwen appeared, having heard that her old friend had come. She led the swordswoman to a place in the inner circle of the camp where she could pitch her tent and rest. Ysbaddaden and Medb watched the two stroll away, and waved when Skatha turned her head and flashed a smile and called something back. Then Medb turned back to her spear practice. She was staring at the target, spear in hand, when Ysbaddaden said, "I have changed, though."

She stayed in her aiming attitude. "I know it well. You've become a hard man."

"That's true. Yet . . . I regret the enmity between us. You were right; I shouldn't have lent my arm to Treon."

She lowered the spear, but didn't look at him. "I, too, have regrets, especially about the way I left you. Too many things had befallen me, and I was too young to understand any of them. No wonder you lost faith in me."

"I've regained it all." He laughed, a huff of breath, and folded his arms over his chest. "I never lost it, really. I knew, from that day to this, we shared a common fate."

To die together? she wondered.

Aloud she said, "To defeat Balor, yes." She lifted

her spear again, and took aim. "To bring the demon out and crush him."

In Balor's cave, Conann stood before his master, who was amusing himself by tossing bits of bloody meat for his hell hounds to snap at. "Lord Balor, we are about to be harassed with the pestilence from Eire."

Balor's face took on sudden white fury. "Impudent fools. They have nothing but sticks and stones to meet my fury. I'll wipe them out."

"You shouldn't waste your time with such trifles, my Lord. Allow me to deal with the vermin. They are struck by madness and the shreds of their mothers' dreams. You shall rule them, as you proved in Omagh."

"Then be swift, Conann." He tossed another scrap of meat for the hounds to yelp and fight over. "I have no patience for these sniveling tribes. Show them Fomor might."

"As you command, my Lord. We shall crush them on the field of battle."

"Take me with you, my Lord Conann!" Dark Indech stepped toward the Evil Eye's throne. "I have reason to meet this Medb again." His axe arm was barely healed from the wound Medb had given him the night of the birth of Gwawl's baby.

Balor laughed heartlessly. "Aye, take him with you, Conann. And take Cethlan, Elanthan, Ethnui, and Octriallach. And Tethra, too."

Conann bowed. "It shall be as you say."

"It shall always be as I say," Balor growled.

In Strabane, as the autumn settled on the mountains, it was a time Medb would never forget. She'd taken the crown of High Ruler while secretly thinking that at any time, if she really wanted to, she could turn her back on Eire, on her position, her responsibilities. If things got too bad, if she grew too exhausted, too desperate, too afraid, she could gather her retainers and simply slink away home to the lush, slow beauty of Connaught, leaving all these troubles to someone else.

She recognized now that such a retreat was an impossibility. There could be no retreat anymore without a triumph first, for her or Balor. The only comfort Connaught could offer her was the knowledge that it was still there. Seeing Omagh, she realized that should she lose the impending struggle, the Evil Eye would turn Connaught into the same desolate emptiness, and she couldn't have borne that. She could bear the thought of her own death more easily.

Thus, finally finding her sticking place, she was mildly surprised to discover how solid it was. And more surprised to find in it a sense of peace. Here was a part of herself that transcended fear, that was brave. Though she didn't want to die, her harshest fears had slipped behind her.

Thus she chose six of the greatest champions in

her composite army to accompany her into battle against Conann. The selection wasn't easy. There were so many willing men and women of exceptional competence and experience. She consulted with her councillors again and again, discussing each prospect's aptitude and dexterity, the level of mastery at spellcasting among the magicians, and the degree of arms skill among the warriors.

Among the most probable Druids were Ceridwen, and yes, fey, aloof Lleflys, and one called Menw, and one called Caradawg, both unknown to Medb but who came to her with high repute. Also Diancecht the Healer. Several bards showed great power: Gwrhyr, Creidhne, and Luchta. Among the array of warriors, the choices were almost too plentiful.

Medb alone made the final selection, because she felt deeply her responsibility to lead the Tuatha de Danann to victory. Anything less meant sentencing their souls to death and deadly night. She listened to the arguments of her councillors but then fell back on her heart. Who inspired the most confidence in her? In whom could she place her trust?

The answers came to her like tears, for those she trusted most were those she loved best: Ysbaddaden, Skatha, and Gwawl; the Archdruid Ceridwen, and silver-bearded Diancecht the Healer; and she also chose the bard Tristan.

These six, she believed, represented the highest level of might and magic in Eire. They would have many weapons–and they would need them all.

The diviners, with their ancient knowledge of the skies, declared that the fifth morning after the pregnant moon was the most favorable time to begin the battle. The day before, Medb and her host tramped through pouring rain to reach the frontiers of Omagh.

When she came out of the trees of Strabane and got her first good look at the devastated province beyond, she couldn't quite grasp what she was seeing. Her eyes had only the experience of the gradual and powerful work of nature, which carves cliffs, erodes mountains, grinds beaches, and moves rocks. Her mind had to piece together by fits and starts this abrupt devastation, unraveling the messages of her eyes. She'd visited Omagh, on the northern coast, several times over the years, but the familiar landmarks seemed deranged and alien, as if she'd strayed across unimaginable distances, over centuries as well as leagues.

"Nuada is no bard," Gwawl, riding at her side, muttered.

He meant the blunt minded warrior's report hadn't come close to describing the devastation of this once beautiful province. Medb spurred her horse to proceed. Every wooded slope had been leveled. She remembered certain fortified villages and towns they should be passing, and the stronghold of Omagh's ancient princes. But there was nothing except flat open expanses where once lodges and farms and byres had stood.

The herd animals had been slaughtered. Omagh had been famous for its fresh goat cheeses. But even the pastures were uprooted. And in the fields, which had been sown with salt, only the occasional severed head on a broken spear grew now.

She tried to keep her mind on necessary thoughts, on the battle wisdom that she had come by so hard, tried to think what strategies would be best since terrain was a negligible factor. Not even a rock pile was left to give her champions tactical advantage.

Toward dusk, her forward scouts came back with news that Conann's encampment was no more than a half-hour's march ahead. Her army had come to the banks of a shallow river. Nuada had said the slaughter was so fearful that the streams were fouled, but a month had passed, and the waters that had flowed red were clear again. She ordered a halt.

Guards were set against lurking Fomors, and shelters raised. Flame-haired, black-garbed Daghda had traveled this far with the army to provide the security, so that the men who must fight on the morrow could rest.

Medb was called out of her tent by him at dusk. His men had found a burned farm lodge where traces of the Fomors' brutality showed in the skeletons of the defenders–bones cut by axe blades, skulls crushed by clubs, spines pierced by spear-barbs. A valuable anklet and toe ring clasped the foot bones of one of the dead, marking him as a person of position. Had this site been the last stand of some champion? Medb ordered the remains of the poor wretches buried where they lay, with all honor. "Build a cairn over their grave," she told Daghda, "to remind all who pass this way of the cruel fate wreaked on them."

She returned to the tent, but lay tense on her straw pallet, burrowed amid woolen blankets and fleecy robes against the season's chill. When she dozed, she had a nightmare: She had defeated Conann, but she couldn't find his Gae Bolga. There was a sense of all for naught, of heavy doom, and heavier grief. She woke in a sweat, and after that she slept not at all. The dream had seemed so clear. She felt it must be a message from Danu to her: Capture the Gae Bolga, at any cost.

The night seemed to last forever, yet when the darkness broke, it was too soon. As Ehtne dressed Medb in her armor, the serving woman's face was pale, her mouth prim and tight. Her wattled throat trembled as she made small noises of distress. Medb shivered, though the morning was mild. She felt her joints aching and her eyes stinging from too little rest. In fact, she felt for the first time her own age. She had lived for twenty-six winters; she was no longer a young woman. All too soon she would be considered one of the elders of her tribe, like Tochmarc. The thought made her long to spend whatever years remained to her in her own citadel, Seamaire, away from all the noise and bustle of this exacting world.

Stepping from her tent, she shaded her eyes to study the blue bowl overhead. The weather was the worst it could be: crystal clear. So much for using strategies that depended on mist or snow, which had proved beneficial to her in other battles.

She spoke a last time with her mages. "Each of you, with your loyal soldiers, will take up a position at the furthest reaches of the battlefield, where you can work your runes without fear of physical attack."

As the sun rose, she heard the reports of scouts who had gone out in the deep of the night, risking their lives to gather information about the Fomors her army would fight today: Tethra, Elathan, Cethlan, Indech, Octriallach, and Ethnui. And, of course, Conann himself.

"At least," Ainle said around a mouthful of crisp, tart apple–his breakfast, "none of them, not even Conann, has any spellcasting capabilities."

The encouragement of this news lasted Medb not quite a breath, for as warriors each of the Fomors mentioned had momentous strength and fortitude, and almost no weaknesses. Medb couldn't name the feelings that swept her when she thought about crossing blades with them. Behind those miserable faces and grotesque bodies, which had terrorized every tribe in Eire for as many years as it had taken her to become High Ruler, was more villainy than she chose to consider. Yet consider it she must.

"They're all champion-level warriors, and every one a depraved devil, totally without honor," Caipre said, speaking Medb's own thoughts.

"All quick, well-armed, and strong," Ainle agreed, swallowing and tossing aside the core of his apple. "And as mean as vipers."

"They've positioned their brawlers beside a hillock–the last hill left in Omagh," added Llugh, ruler-warrior from Tara. "You'll see them soon after you cross the river."

Medb left off conferring, and stepped into her chariot, and nodded to her driver. She would speak to her soldiers before she sent them to their fates. The regiments had drawn up along the little river. As she rode along the line, a damp wind buffeted her face. She felt this moment was beyond bombast and bravado, so she spoke simply. "We are a match for any army, but there will be lives lost today. The holy men and women tell us the human soul is indestructible. Certainly, the human spirit is, or we would not be here, willing to make the sacrifices we are about to make.

"I salute each of you for your courage, and I pray to the Goddess that together we can save our sacred soil."

She sensed they'd expected more from her, something stirring and eloquent.

She glimpsed Ysbaddaden, at the head of his own regiment. In the past few days he'd grown quieter, nervier, more inward. He didn't seem afraid–he was the only absolutely fearless man she'd ever met–but here at last was the hour on which all his thoughts and ambitions had been set for so long. Would he find gratification in it?

Please, Danu, let us all find reason to revel in the hours ahead.

To the sound of faint horns, the army started into motion. They crossed the river and the bare earth beyond. Medb unsheathed her sword and took a firm grip on her charmed shield.

She spied the small rise Llugh had described. Along the left of it, a meager rank of Fomor beasts and giants stood with Elathan, one of the most intelligent of his race, and not so repulsive as some in his appearance. He shouted, "A wise word to the fool who claims the crown of High Ruler! Many a Fomor bludgeon will drink human blood this hour!"

Despite his bold words, the brutes he stood with seemed to sense the doom Medb felt, for there was no brandishing of the clubs and cudgels and bows that served as their weapons. They stood silent, almost like condemned beings, shifting from foot to foot as the human infantry advanced at a plodding march toward them.

Medb felt a prickle of presentiment. This was too easy, too obvious. What was Conann up to? Where were his other champions? Possibilities pecked at her like a flock of attacking birds. The brutes of the exposed battalion looked even more slow-witted and stupid than most Fomor soldiers.

All at once she realized, and shouted over her shoulder, "The main force is drawn up behind the hill!"

It was plain to her now. Conann's scheme was for her to become embroiled with these dullards, which he intended to sacrifice as so much blade-fodder; then, as she grew flushed with easy triumph, he would send his better troops in an abrupt flanking assault. He'd assumed Medb wouldn't deduce such a simple stratagem. He was wrong.

"Ignore these brutes! Charge over the knoll! That's where the real army is!"

The infantry, heartened to feel she'd regained her leadership, picked up speed. The battle horns sounded, now profoundly resonant. The army started a running charge headlong over the hillock, where they surprised the hidden Fomors.

Heroic was the clash of that meeting, and titanic was the struggle that followed. The hidden reserves, caught unawares, were driven into the ranks of the simpletons positioned alongside the hill, who in turn became so flustered that they struck out against their own kind. In their confusion, their bowmen overshot. Others stood stunned, unable to fight or flee. Jostled and panicked, the brutes were thrown into a melee as Medb's champions and veterans cut them down like trees in a forest. Great wails rose to the monster who had enslaved them, and their foul tears fell like rain.

Medb witnessed the work of the bard, Tristan, as

a giant beast bearing down on her chariot was engulfed in a cloud of poison smoke. Even as the creature screamed his outrage, a burning flood of poison poured into his nostrils and gaping mouth, choking him.

A hundred yards away, Gwawl's opponent stepped on an invisible firetrap set by one of the Druids. The brute's wild hair and animal-skin clothing exploded into flames. The air around him grew so hot that five more Fomor died by inhaling it. The onrushing blaze spread into a tornado of flames that caught and killed four more.

Yet despite this first triumph, this was the most uncertain, courage-straining war Medb had yet conducted. Within that first hour, the bright shields of her grand host were hacked, their splendid colors nicked. Honed spears grew notched and dull. Colorful tunics became tattered and stained with both green and red blood. Many men were forced to retreat from the field, breathing harshly and bearing horrific wounds.

Medb directed her chariot driver into the midst of the fight, where she supposed she would find the skulking Conann. But he was nowhere to be seen. With the thunder of her own blood in her ears, she at last spied him–at a safe distance from the bloodshed, waiting like a coiled reptile. She felt a chill, sensing that he had tricked her after all.

Yes, she knew it as she knew the tumult of her own heart. She saw his champions closing in on her. They seemed to get past her own three champions as if they didn't exist. The full weight of her danger hit her. Conann had meant for her to guess his stratagem of using the hillock as a blind. While she'd been congratulating herself on how she'd frustrated his plan, he'd used her own cleverness against her. And now he meant to go for her jugular. He'd ordered his best champions to go for her and only her. She saw Cethlan, Ethnui, and her most recent foe, the giant, Indech, his arm apparently healed. She turned her head and there were Octriallach and Tethra, too.

Still in her chariot, she took a firmer grip on her enchanted shield. But no matter what magic she had on her side, it wouldn't hold off the forces squeezing down on her. She saw with mortal terror that there was no way of halting the Fomor champions. They were coming, and they were coming for her.

Ysbaddaden, fighting a brute with a gobbling, outraged face almost at her chariot wheel, swung Answerer with an expression that told her that the *something* he felt in battle was singing like music in his blood. His charmed sword, so strong and sharp it could bisect a leaf floating in midair, felled brutes right and left. But when he turned his head to Medb, her face must have mirrored her thoughts, for he sobered, looked about to see the Fomors bearing down on her, and shouted, "Move! Get out of here! Make them come after you!"

As she nodded to her charioteer, she heard the gobbling Fomor he was fending off begin a shrill keening. A glance back confirmed that he'd made another kill.

CHAPTER TEN

Flight then became Medb's tactic. When Octriallach, missing several fangs in his frog-like face, came too close, she shouted for her driver to whip up her horses and move her to safety. Her faithful warriors followed, battling back the pursuing brutes all the way. The good blades of her champions did what they could to reduce the numbers of the horde chasing her, and her mages, placed out of harm's way, endured no interference. Safe in their separate locations, they targeted the monsters again and again with their most devastating spells.

The Fomors were hit by hurling stones and speeding fireballs. When Cethlan broke free of Medb's defenders, Medb felt a sudden tingling on her skin, as in the seconds before thunder breaks. The hair stirred on her sweaty arms and on the nape of her neck, lifted by a rush of unseen energy. Then, amidst a powerful barrage of sound, bolts of lightning crashed down with a succession of booms. They formed burning blue-white cages around at least two dozen of Cethlan's brutish soldiers. When they vanished as quickly as they'd arrived, Cethlan snarled, "You've burned my soldiers! You'll pay for that, I promise you!" His grotesque face was a mask of bridled fury. Medb shuddered to see how the light fell on his eyes, making them look all pupil, all emptiness.

But the spell had given her time to find a way out of the melee again. Her glimpse of Cethlan's eyes was a departing glimpse. Again, the enemy must expend time and strength to catch her.

Lightning was the most devastating offense, as the distant rune-casters soon discovered. Inexplicably, the Fomor champions paid no heed to Medb's mages, and even ignored the danger of the fatal spells themselves unless they were personally knocked down. Clawing, scratching, slavering, they continued to close in on Medb. The worst among their soldiers looked as if they hadn't eaten for days, and Medb began to wonder if their commanders had starved them–and promised them her for their next meal!

When about half the enemy forces had fallen, her charioteer was cut down by a vicious club blow. Medb leaped free of the now useless vehicle. Without a spare word, Ysbaddaden, Gwawl, and Skatha surrounded her.

"We have to cut a way through to Conann! We have to capture the Gae Bolga!"

The Fomors, meanwhile, continued their mindless quest. From the corner of her eye, Medb saw Gwawl embroiled in combat against Indech. Gwawl seemed wonderfully strong today, no doubt the effect of his Stone of Might, but as he lifted his shield to parry the Fomor's axe, Cethlan hewed him from behind. Medb's oldest friend folded and fell.

Skatha leaped to back the beasts away from the fallen warrior, who lay bleeding on the field. Medb fought her way to him, and as her champions and soldiers surrounded her, she knelt to remove Gwawl's helmet and take his fair head in her lap. She cried out to see the extent of his wounds.

His eyes were shut; he seemed dead already. His neck had been slashed, and his heart's blood gushed from the wound. His ruddy cheeks were already ash-white.

Diancecht, swathed in his undyed woolen robe, came as if from nowhere and knelt beside Medb, his eyes shining from the shadowy cavern of his priest's hood. He had given himself the glamour of a warrior, and had a sword in his hand. The air crackled with the magic forces he had gathered about him.

Medb, who had been taught from her earliest years to show any Druid the greatest deference, nonetheless issued a harsh order. "They call you Healer–heal him!"

But Diancecht shook his head in sorrow. Flinging back his hood, he said, "There's nothing I can do. Alas, these wounds are too serious."

Gwawl's eyelids fluttered, opened, and he looked up at Medb through clouded eyes. "My hour has come." His voice was like the papery whisper of arid leaves.

"No, Gwawl, you mustn't say that."

"I'm so tired. So weary. Let me go, Medb. I need to go."

Tears choked her. "Don't. What would I do without you?"

He fought to draw another breath. "Live," he whispered.

"No. This isn't–"

"*Shh* . . . " He managed to lift a hand to gesture her to silence. "Can you hear them?"

"Hear what, my friend?"

"They call me to join them." His eyes cleared as he looked at Medb. "Take care of Li Ban and my children. I leave all my hopes in your keeping. Only you can free Eire."

"Don't go," she pleaded.

But neither her command nor all her heart's desire could hold him. Like candles burned to their ends, the lights in his eyes guttered and died. His face went lax, as if he heard some blissful choir, some music more alluring than anything this earth offered. Medb spoke his name, stroked his cheek. He gave no sign of hearing. In her throat a hot swell ripened. She swallowed it down and spoke his name again. But it had no effect at all.

She knew grief would fall on her like a storm in the time to come, but for now she had no time for it. The swords and axes clanging almost above her head recalled her to who and what she was, and what she was chosen to do. She closed the eyes of her old friend, and laid him back on the bloodied ground with all gentleness. As she stood, it broke her heart to see that his hair still burned on his head like a gilt helmet.

She paused to draw breath. And it surprised her that the light that had been as pleasant as a well-worn shawl this morning was fading. The first chill of evening had fallen. The entire day had passed her in a blur of butchery and carnage. She looked around, filled with more purpose than ever. Where was that fiend, Conann?

Her eyes found him not far away, and saw that he was choking with laughter. "So, you lost your dear companion! Will you lose yourself, too, my Lady High Ruler?"

Gwawl was dead. And he didn't mind. Gwawl was dead. The air touching Medb's face felt charged and thick, as though there had been a silent detonation, which in fact there had been–a corrosive blast of rage and strength.

"Come and be my bride, Medb! Yield to me and you need not die! Come to me and even now you need not die!"

Ysbaddaden nor Skatha nor Diancecht paid heed to the monster. They were too busy slashing and cutting. Ysbaddaden's radiant sword seemed intent on nothing but carving a path right through what little remained of that strange golden day, carving a way closer and closer to his oldest adversary.

Medb followed his flashing blade with a determination that for once doubled his. The four of them cleared away Conann's very bodyguards. And then they crossed blades with the monster himself.

"Your day has come," the Fomor growled. He

scorned using a shield, and wielded the thrusting Gae Bolga in the hand that didn't brandish his heavy battle axe.

"Brave words for one facing defeat," Medb answered, her magical shield fending off yet another bone-shivering blow.

They might have fought for days, for weeks. Medb lost track of how long it took to wear him down. Now and again, as she tired, she felt a spell flooding her with strength and resolution. She sensed it was the same for Ysbaddaden and Skatha, and imagined Ceridwen's long spidery fingers spread out against the air.

"You surprise me," Conann panted, speaking to Medb alone. "I doubted you would last this long."

"The time has come to settle the score between us, and to do that I can last until the moon no longer chases the sun."

"Don't get your hopes up. Our contest is far from over!"

But as strong as Conann was, he couldn't fight off four of them, not forever. Ysbaddaden wove his bright sword in a way that caused Conann's spear-arm to fly wild. The Gae Bolga clattered out of his grasp. As he registered this calamity, Skatha lunged with her sword, piercing his side.

He fell back, but didn't fall. Instead, he turned, and began to run. One of his own fallen brutes tripped him. He went to his knees, screaming in frustration. That was when Medb had her chance and took it. She spread her feet for good purchase, and took a firm, two-handed grip on her sword. She swung it around in a swift stroke, deft and deadly. The level plane of her blade cut through his corded neck as if through a loaf of bread. His severed head toppled from his shoulders like a stone, and the monster himself slumped forward, crashed to ruin, and lay crumpled on the earth, dead.

Dead! The word caroled in her. Dead! She had seldom known such relief.

But from the corner of her eye she saw Ysbaddaden's face, naked, hungry with envy, and so vulnerable that she closed her eyes.

When she opened them, he'd recovered. She asked, "Where is the spear?" She ran to where she thought it had fallen, but it wasn't there. Her nightmare seemed to be coming true. She must have the Gae Bolga! Her dream had warned her that without it, this struggle would end in appalling defeat, for both Medb and for all Eire.

She heard a cheer, and looked up from her frenzied search to see that the Fomors remaining on the battlefield seemed elated. She scanned the horizon–and soon knew why they took such heart.

The victorious tribesmen thrust up their hacked shields to prove how bravely they had fought. They flaunted their wounds, and wiped the greenish Fomor blood off their thrusting spears as if impatient to use them again. But then, like Medb, they heard a cry sounding out of the north, a cry terrible and fearful to hear.

"The Gae Bolga! Where is it!" Medb crouched with Ysbaddaden to roll Conann's headless body. "Not beneath him!"

As she stood, panic darkened her mind, and out of that blackness she heard Gwawl speak . . . yet the voice seemed strange, recalling some other voice she had known, too: Danu's. *There, Medb, to your left, between those two rocks.*

She staggered to her feet and spun around–and spied the smallest glint of brightness, the tip of one of the spear's many barbs.

At the same instant, the swollen sun set and darkness gathered like a shadow over the battlefield. And as if from the depths of that darkness, Balor rode up on a great steed out of a depression Medb hadn't seen before in that featureless landscape. He wore his helmet with its great curved horns. Surrounding him were his horse hounds, fangs glinting and snapping at the very air, and his foot hounds, Fomor brutes, shrieking villainous giants, brandishing razor-sharp axes and heavy, black maces.

Medb had almost forgotten how malicious the monster was. Fortune had betrayed him for an hour, and the world had turned against him, but now Medb felt her victory sliding from her grasp even as she extended her hand to seize Conann's spear.

Balor's steed dashed for the same cleft of rock. As

Medb grasped the spear's haft, she was attacked by one of the monster's hounds. The spear clattered away as the hound hit her directly in the chest, snapping at her face. She fell onto her back with its weight, and covered her face and curled her body against the dripping fangs. Meanwhile, Balor proved his arm was still long. Bent in his saddle, muscles bulging, he swept up the deadly weapon.

He was still in command, still wielding his great power–and now he had the Gae Bolga, perhaps the only weapon that could destroy him. Medb and her cause were doomed.

The hound clawing and snapping at Medb suddenly yelped and left off tearing at her sleeves and hands. Ysbaddaden gutted it with his sword.

"Who dares to meddle with my fighting pets?" Balor screamed.

"I do!" Ysbaddaden stood tall and threatening above Medb, guarding her from two other animals that would have attacked except for the eerie radiance of his witchy blade. "And my Answerer cries to taste your blood as well!"

He was taking the monster's attention off Medb. At a distance, Balor brought his great horse to a rearing halt. His followers grouped around him, including those left from Conann's defeat. Flaunting the spear he had stolen from her very fingertips, he cried, "I see you have been led astray by Medb, and by her Goddess's mists and her priests' wizardries."

"Led astray? I think not! She and her Goddess and her wizards killed your lieutenant this day. We'll kill you next."

"You think you can kill *me?*"

Medb rose to her knees to stop Ysbaddaden from inciting him further. "His eye!" she warned Ysbaddaden. "Don't test him!"

"Look how you cower!" he scoffed at Medb. "Because you know you'll never win over me. Nonetheless, it amuses me to watch you try. Come to Tory Island, my Lady High Ruler." He made the title sound ridiculous. She *knew* it was ridiculous, kneeling there in the dust of her ruin.

"We'll come!" Ysbaddaden shouted.

Balor glanced at him again. "Would you like a morsel of what I fed Medb's father, warrior?" He opened his evil eye. At once, Medb felt Ysbaddaden weaken and fold. She leaped to protect him. But Balor shut his eye again, and threw his head back, and laughed. The sound was like the chime of steel.

He swept his one-eyed gaze around at her army. To a man, they recoiled. Loud enough to be heard from one end of the field to the other, he bellowed, "Terror and ruin, slaughter and blood, the rage of heaven and hell I carry with me. I will curse all your banners to the third and fourth generations. Dare not take up weapons and arms against me again, or ruin will strike you wherever my sight may reach."

His horse reared again; its hooves pawed the

darkened air as he spurred it back in the direction from which he'd come, toward the sea, Medb guessed, where he no doubt had boats waiting to return him to the safety of his Tory Island stronghold. But before he could quite disappear from sight, Ceridwen began to chant. Her long-fingered hands shaped the air, and something hot and molten materialized within that shape. Her hands didn't seem to feel the heat of it as she threw the substance, which looked like molten lava, directly at Balor's retreating back. With a shushing boom it sped toward him, and hit him squarely. He threw his arms out in pain, and the Gae Bolga spun out of his grasp. Skatha raced to retrieve it, Ysbaddaden hard on her heels, to hack at any hound or brute who tried to stop her.

Screaming in fright, Balor's horse carried its rider on, and the two disappeared into the depression from which they'd emerged.

Again the victorious army cheered. But not Medb. Hands and arms bleeding from innumerable dog bites, she climbed to her feet and walked like a sleepwalker through the broken blades and splintered shields of the battlefield. She dragged one foot after the other through the day's slain, blinking like an owl, until she looked down once more on Gwawl's fair face.

The exhausted soldiers and champions returned to their encampment. Medb came on a pallet made of lashed shields, for the poisonous slaver of the hound that had bitten her festered in her wounds immediately. Li Ban met her, and asked softly, "And where is my husband? Where is Gwawl?"

Around them, there was talk and even some weary laughter among the soldiers who naturally were glad to still be alive. But there was grief too, for many had not lived through that terrible day.

Skatha took on the burden of telling Li Ban. "He gave his life. We are the better off for his sacrifice, and the worse off for his death."

Li Ban took the news quietly. Though Medb was very ill through the night, she refused to stay abed when Gwawl was put to his rest the following day. Still pale and shaken, she stood by pyre built of the broken spear shafts of yesterday's victory. Medb clasped silent Li Ban's hand as Bran cleared his throat to speak, paused, and cleared it once more. He had known Gwawl since joining Medb's service after the Destruction, and in the end, was too overcome to speak.

Seeing he couldn't find the needed words, Caipre, the bard, began: "Noble men, brave women, with a heavy heart I speak of sorrow. Our Lady and her forces fought valiantly, but Conann and his devil's brood were too hale for Gwawl. Alas, fate threw our warrior's lot to the foe, and left us with misery in the midst of our victory. Yet death has no finality. And hope never dies."

Gwawl's brothers-in-arms, Ainle and Daghda,

stepped forward with blazing torches and set the pyre ablaze. Li Ban remained silent and motionless, but Medb muffled a cry to see her oldest companion engulfed by those flames.

Once his body was consecrated, a hole was dug among the roots of an oak. There Gwawl's ashes would sleep forever, clasped by the sacred tree. The funerary urn, painted with eyes and coils, was reverently returned to the Earth's womb. It was an honor for the warrior Gwawl; usually only Druids were given to the oaks. The warrior began his journey to the Otherworld with all the articles he might need. Medb had ordered that his grave should contain even fine silverwork and other treasures. She and Li Ban were the last to leave his grave site, and then Medb turned away, too. Gwawl's wife must be grieving even more deeply than Medb. How did she bear it? No wonder she seemed stunned into silence.

Despite Medb's success in Omagh, she still stood a long way from a final victory over Balor. For that reason, neither she nor her heroes could spend time on lengthy triumphs. They had the Gae Bolga; they'd thrown the Fomors into doubt of their powers; and now they must hurry to exploit the new situation. Consulting with her council, she chose Llud to replace Gwawl.

One month after Conann's death, after Balor had stumbled back to his desolate outpost over the sea,

Medb and her champions and armies traveled to a squalid little fishing village under a sheer sea cliff. Here a few of Omagh's scarce refugees were trying to reconstruct their old lives. Bidding farewell to faithful wives and affectionate mothers, the soldiers boarded a flotilla of boats and set out on a sea shining like hammered metal toward a darkness gloomier than night.

Medb's boat was small but sound as a walnut. She sat in the high stern beside Tochmarc, who was slumped over asleep. Li Ban stood in the bow where she seemed not to notice the spray that splashed her each time the prow dug into the waves. The shining sheaf of Fann's hair obscured one eye as she sat beside a raw-boned, dour soldier and smiled politely at his exaggerated heroics. Matth stifled a yawn, for it was many hours since any of them had slept.

She had brought along these councillors, these devoted friends, not to go ashore and fight with her, but to serve as witnesses to whatever would happen on the morrow. If she and her champions were destroyed, someone must warn Eire.

The tremendous figure of Ysbaddaden strode up and down the center aisle between the two sets of oarsmen. The other champions were in different boats, but Ysbaddaden insisted on staying at Medb's side. As she rose from her seat, he stopped short and stiffened, as tense as a lion crouched to pounce. Blocking her way, he said in a low and dreadful voice, worse than any roar of rage, "Well?"

Medb couldn't answer him. Instead, she said, "Let me pass, please. I want to speak to Li Ban."

After a moment, he did as she asked, and she made her way between the oarsmen, past the piles of shields, swords, sheathed axe heads, mail, and helmets, to the lone woman in the bow.

Medb didn't know how to comfort her. Now and again she had tried, but no words could pierce her friend's grief. She didn't try today. Instead, feeling Ysbaddaden's eyes on her back, she looked over her shoulder at his anxious, stalwart figure–and met his stare, dark in the late afternoon sun. She turned away again, blinded by that look.

She put her hand on Li Ban's shoulder. "I don't know what to tell Ysbaddaden."

Li Ban glanced over her shoulder, too, and said indifferently, "He's dangerous. He's lost his perspective. Killing Balor has become an obsession with him."

Medb heard a stir behind her. The captain had decided there was enough wind to allow the oarsmen to rest their backs. The mast was being stepped in. It set the rigging all taut. Then sail was furled. The wind caught it with a *whump!* Both Medb and Li Ban reached for the rail as the bow skewed to the right. But soon the boat seemed to fly over the crests of the high, plumed sea.

"Won't you come sit down?" Medb asked.

"You go ahead; I'm fine." Li Ban patted Medb's

hand.

Able to do her friend no good, Medb went back to her place, side by side with sleeping Tochmarc high in the stern. Ysbaddaden, growling under his breath, sat as well, next to Matth; yet there was no relaxation in the lines of his body.

The sun lowered in the west, so low that the heaves of the ocean blocked it. Medb sat in the shadow of the big sail, where the light grew as muted as evening. Tochmarc continued to sleep.

Ysbaddaden said to Matth, "We should land as soon as we find the island."

Matth shook his head. "It's best to wait till daybreak and go in with a belly full of decent food and a good night's sleep. Remember, the few reports we have indicate the landing won't be easy. We don't want to risk that in the dark."

Ysbaddaden made a motion with his shoulders that said he didn't need food and sleep, that he was used to taking risks. Over the past month he'd reduced himself to an isolated element, a single purpose, stripping off every layer of friendship and connection, leaving only the naked need to kill Balor. It was a need so strong that Medb feared it left him vulnerable rather than strong. Li Ban was right, he was dangerous. He was a ship that had lost its rudder and was veering wildly in the winds. He'd lost all regard for safety, and there was nothing more dangerous than that.

The question he wanted Medb to answer was

who would be the one to wield the Gae Bolga. He wanted her to say it was him. He wanted to give the monster of Tory Island his end. He wanted to lift Balor's head on the thirty points of the deadly pike–and that was all he wanted.

When Tochmarc rose to stretch his legs, Ysbaddaden moved next to Medb. "You'll give it to me in the morning?" When she didn't answer, he lost what little patience he had left. "Oh, by the sun, why are you arguing!"

She, Skatha, and Ysbaddaden had all practiced with the spear during past weeks. Llud had tried to throw it, too, but quickly gave up in frustration. Medb was hardly any better than he was, but she persisted, trying again and again to learn the method, which required using one's foot.

Ysbaddaden got so he could hit the straw target twice out of every three tries. His skill and speed, and the fire of his concentration, were hardly matched even by Skatha, whose record was one bull's-eye out of three. Medb did less well. Nonetheless, she'd already decided she must wield the weapon herself.

She hadn't told anyone because she knew Ysbaddaden, and maybe Skatha, too, would quarrel with her decision. But it seemed the moment couldn't be postponed any longer.

"No, Ysbaddaden, I won't give the Gae Bolga to you."

"Why not?"

She couldn't think how to tell him without injuring him. She strained to understand what he felt, but couldn't; it baffled her. "There's something in you that just doesn't know when to quit, Ysbaddaden. You don't understand limits; you're blind to boundaries."

He stared at her as if she were speaking gibberish.

"Whatever drives you, it's beyond courage, beyond spirit. It made me leave you behind when I left Ben Skellig. And it makes you unfit to wield the Gae Bolga today."

She couldn't look at him. She stared out at the vast expanse of water. The wind calmed as dusk approached. A dark purple sky veiled the horizon. The last arrow of sun blazoned the sails of the flotilla and then was gone. The ocean steadied almost at once.

Li Ban, still in the bow, cried out suddenly, "There it is!"

Everyone rose and peered where she pointed. Medb pushed through, trying to get to the bow. Fann, she saw in a passing glance, looked nauseous. Was she a poor sailor, made ill by the heaving water, or was she simply sickened from nerves? The soldier beside her muttered a prayer, "Danu, let our honor preserve and brace us."

Edging in beside Li Ban, Medb got her first glimpse of Tory Island, motionless amid the froth and roil of the endless waves lapping its shores. Aside from its formidable locale, it had a rocky, unprotected coast and a mountainous cragged interior.

"Then Skatha–you're going to give it to Skatha." Ysbaddaden's voice, coming from behind Medb, broke into her thoughts.

She felt a sharp retort freeze on her tongue. It took effort to shake milder words loose. "I can't ask anything of Skatha, or of you, that I can't ask of myself."

Whatever she'd expected, it wasn't what she heard: "Then you're a fool, Princess–and you're going to damn us all to rout and ruin."

Others, hearing him speak so to the High Ruler of Eire, gasped. Or muttered. Or cursed. Depending on their natures. Li Ban stood in motionless shock. Tochmarc's expression slackened.

"You go too far, Ysbaddaden." Medb answered him in a cold, even voice. "You always go too far. Were your character in other respects equal to your boldness, your energy–" Recalling the ominous black rock rising out of the sea behind her, she left off. And began again. "We shouldn't squabble, you and I. We've been through too much together. There was a time when you led and I followed trustingly. I'm asking you to do the same now. Follow my lead, Ysbaddaden, for on the morrow I shall need you at my back."

Anchored offshore, Medb watched the last light lower on the spires and pinnacles of Tory Island's lofty skyline. She pulled her cloak closer for warmth as a delicate land breeze wandered down from the heights of the interior, bringing a sweet smell of thriving forests. Medb wondered that such a Fomor place should have such a sweet smell.

Stars came out in the cloudless sky, and a thin golden crescent of moon sent a feeble track of light over the ocean. On the island, bonfires bloomed in three or four places. What was happening around those fires? Something horrible, no doubt. Yet the combination of wood smoke and Mother Earth remained the sweetest of all smells.

Medb sat with her back against the stern gunwales, and eventually heard a faint lift of song drift from Tristan's boat. The distant breakers shattering against the island's stone cliffs made a murmuring undertone to the bard's melancholy singing.

When the sliver of moon set, all along the shore marched the flare of innumerable torches. Medb and her boat mates spoke in low voices, all peering toward the dark loom of the island. Medb overheard snatches of talk from the other boats as well. Tochmarc yawned, and said with heavy eyes, "They're getting ready for you, my Lady."

As the sky lightened, she saw the boats had drifted some distance west during the night. Here, the surf spurted up sheer black cliffs. As the coppery-gold sun touched the island's tallest summit, the moments seemed to slip away from Medb faster and faster.

The light grew stronger, and the captains weighed their anchors and took the boats around to where they had seen the torches earlier. It seemed to be the only landing point, though not a good one. The sea broke sharply on a long curving beach of pebbles. Up from this steep shore stood a dense array of club-wielding Fomor soldiers. Between their ranks darted crazed human slavewomen, naked or dressed in scraps, waving smoking brands like mad furies. The sight of these poor wretches reminded Medb that she could have been among them.

One of the women ran down to the surf with a tattered, blackened cloak. She thrust it in the water as if to wash it. Medb saw bruises on her face and her thin arms, layered shades of purple and yellow. With a voice shriller than the gulls wheeling above, she wailed "Medb . . . Medb . . ." as she lifted the cloak from the sea. It streamed with blood.

Fann cried, "A *bain sidhe!*"

"A trick, no doubt!" Matth scoffed.

Still, everyone knew that a bain sidhe's wail portended death.

As the boats moved in, champions and soldiers alike armed themselves. Voices were nearly drowned in the roar of the great, high surf. Medb scanned the lines of the defenders and saw the Fomor champions: the brawny female, Domnu; Morc, armed with the stolen Sword of Nuada; clever, almost-human Bress; pointy-eared, evil Clach; stupid and repulsive Eochaid; and mighty Ruadan.

Where was Balor? Li Ban, moving to stand by Medb, said, "Do you suppose he's hiding somewhere up there?" She pointed to the high contours of the land.

"No." Medb licked at the sea salt on her lips, for she had spied her enemy. Balor stood above the line of brutes, on a tolerably flat shelf of ground at the base of the tallest mountain. He wore his horned helmet over his flat beastly face, and his every line, even his grinning grimace, seemed to say, Come on!

"He seems as hale and hearty as ever," Ysbaddaden said dryly.

"Recovered from Omagh, yes." The dawning sun behind them, the boats drew nearer the landing spot. Medb gazed forward with her emotions focused. Closer in, the mountains rose in fantastic spires and turrets wooded to the tops. Innumerable waterfalls plunged over crags, hanging like suspended strands of silver, sharply visible against the background of dark green. The sloping terrain was sure to hinder the army's movement. If only Medb had a hope of bad weather, of fog, in which her soldiers might hide if need be.

Her boat would be the first to land. Dressed in her armor, she gripped her shield and sword. The Gae Bolga was strapped to her back. She muttered, "Danu, thank you for Your great goodness toward me, and please, bless me with a little more of it today."

The captain, gripping the heavy steering oar, gave a shout, and every oar shoveled into the water. As the boat tore through the waves toward the landing point, the captain shouted again. The oarsmen ceased. Three . . . four . . . five waves broke under the boat. The dense throng of Fomors standing above the shore awaited the arrivals with taunts and dares. Many of them beat their breasts. Suddenly the captain gripped the haft of the steering oar strongly and yelled, "Row! Here is a great wave! Row!"

The oarsmen bent to their work, grunting with effort. The boat shot forward, and then heaved high in the air on a wave larger than the others. The vessel raced for the pebbled shore. The captain held them stern-on with efforts that made his arm muscles bulge. The boat sped far up the beach.

Medb breathed hard, as if she were rowing, too. Then she felt a sensation take her. Her breathing changed, slowed, deepened. A quiet vibration filled her as strength poured into her.

A spell sent by one of her mages.

Four soldiers left their oars and sprang over the rail into the wave breaking on the steep beach. They dug their feet into the stones and held the vessel against the backward wash. The rest of the soldiers raised a cheer as the wave receded, then they too sprang out and ran to the high-water line.

Stepping ashore, Medb's body throbbed like a plucked bowstring. All around her the charged air hummed as she and Ysbaddaden followed their soldiers up the beach. The emptied boat backed away, and Ceridwen's boat landed. Llud, Diancecht, Tristan, and Skatha all one by one sprang over the bulwarks of their boats, along with their soldiers and all their martial equipment.

Chapter Eleven

Medb felt relieved to see that the human slavewomen had disappeared from among the Fomor ranks. They might be mad but they weren't oblivious to danger. Now nothing stood between her and Balor but these Fomor brutes. She felt a wild, ruthless exuberance. Without waiting further, she gave a cry and started up the slope, heading straight for the nearest great, dumb-looking beast. The Fomor wore a helmet that made his face seem all swarthy shadow. Killing him, Medb knew suddenly what Ysbaddaden felt in battle. Ecstasy swept through her in a seething blood-red tide.

At first, the Fomors defended the steep slope easily. Again and again Medb heard the swish of a club descending and the scream of a man whose skull was crushed. Beside her a fellow fell clutching at his belly, his weapon spinning harmlessly into the sea. He dropped to the pebbles, gave a jerk that spasmed his whole body, then was still.

On that steep battleground, as the bodies fell, they tumbled back into the ranks of the fighters below, disheartening them. Tristan took care of that by casting powerful spells to increase the morale of the champions and their soldiers. And now and again Medb saw a twisting flash of light sent down on the enemy by Ceridwen and Diancecht. Slowly, slowly, the army began to cut its way up through the blocking enemy ranks. Slowly, they climbed to Balor's height, from which he had not moved.

Another hour passed, and more corpses lay in piles under the Fomors' clubs. Medb sustained a cut to her knee, and paused to have it dressed behind the lines. Llud came to report. Leaning breathless on his sword, he said, "Balor's taken up his stance between two impassable bogs. It's a strategic spot. Only a single company at a time can confront him directly from the south. To the north, that harridan from hell, Domnu, has set up a rear guard, preventing access from that direction."

As the strongest of the warrior-class Fomors, Domnu no doubt hoped to take Conann's old post as Balor's tax collector and Eire's general bane. If Medb didn't win today, the hell-bitch surely would get her wish. But how could Medb win if she couldn't get a clear shot at Balor with the Gae Bolga?

Sorcery was in order. The spellcasters must carry the burden of reducing Balor's strength.

As soon as she rejoined the battle, the monster's evil eye found her, and proved ruinous. From such a distance he couldn't kill her outright, as he had her father, but he wreaked four times the damage of any offensive spell cast by Medb's Druids and bard. From that moment on, if she took a blow from a Fomor, Balor's evil eye was sure to sweep in right behind.

She resorted to making the Fomors chase her

around in circles. With Llud and Ysbaddaden at her side, she played the game of Omagh all over again, the game of defend and retreat.

Balor, incensed by her tactic, cried in his booming voice, "*Medb, you can't run from me! Nor can you be protected!*" He turned his evil eye toward her guardians. Ysbaddaden faltered; Llud stumbled. Balor put his hands together over his horned helmet and shook them as he laughed, "*All your far-reaching schemes go down this day! And all your companions, too.*"

With that, he turned his evil eye on her. She went to her knees, and couldn't seem to rise, even when Balor's attention fell elsewhere. Thankfully, he couldn't afford to aim every barrage of his life-sapping glare at her.

She felt another spell of sorcery surround her. It felt like a skin-prickling rain. Her spirit seemed to spiral up–enough for her to climb to her feet again. Looking about her, her soldiers also had a more vigorous demeanor.

While she, Llud, and Ysbaddaden tried to kill as many Fomors as possible, she dispatched Skatha and her forces to attack the brutes guarding Balor's rear. Meanwhile, her mages kept trouncing away at the Fomors guarding him. The villain behaved as if he couldn't care less. He continued by rote to cast his hideous eye at one invading champion after another.

The mages did what they could to restore the warriors after each blast of that diabolic eye, but they concentrated mostly on Balor himself, and after many an hour, his vitality at last seemed to wane. He staggered–and the expression on his grimacing face showed utter bewilderment at this weakening. Medb saw that change in him and, leaving Llud to keep the monster aware of his power to the south, she and Ysbaddaden began to work their way around the marsh northwest of him.

It was the longest trek of her life. Her soldiers went down one after another. Seeing men she cared about fall, she grew angry. Then she heard a sound like a gong, and the hair lifted on her arms and neck as she saw several of her fallen rise up alive again. A corpse almost at her feet opened its eyes, moved, and stood up as if lifted by strings.

What chilling spell of necromancy was this?

She had no time to ponder it, for finally she and Ysbaddaden rounded the bog and met with Skatha's forces. The swordswoman had a crust of dried blood below one ear when Medb paused to give her new orders. "There's only room for one of us to attack these guards, so we'll do it in rotation, getting what rest and what help we can from the mages."

Ysbaddaden didn't like the plan. She saw it in his face. And in a sudden and unreasonable move, he rushed the Fomors.

Ysbaddaden felt it was all taking too long. How much more could Medb–or any of them–take from that evil eye? They were going to lose, and Balor's hordes would again invade Eire. A bold move was needed–but Medb didn't make bold moves. It was up to Ysbaddaden.

Making up his mind, he dashed forward. He felt no dread or foreboding, only the galvanic excitement of confronting his opponent at last. It was almost like an electric charge. "For Eire!" he shouted, trying to slash the nearest Fomor and slip by him at the same time.

It didn't work. He felt a fearful blow. A stitch of pain tore through his back like a bolt of lightning. He barely kept his hold on Answerer as he fell.

Medb watched Ysbaddaden try to drive right through the squeeze of Fomors, and she saw brawny, clever Domnu swivel and hack at him with her axe from behind. Before the fiend could finish off her victim, however, a fierce wind hit her and blew her back from Ysbaddaden. The wind shrieked in Medb's ears. Tristan's work. He'd placed the very winds of the Earth on her side. The powerful gusts buffeted Domnu right into the marsh, where she floundered, thrashing and slapping the surface in a panic.

"Quicksand! I can't get free! Master, I'm sinking! My lord Balor!"

Her master showed her no sympathy. Nor did any of the brutes on more certain ground cast her more than an indifferent glance. They had no time, for Ysbaddaden's soldiers didn't see their leader go down without rushing to defend him. Skatha dashed as well, and lifting Ysbaddaden's upper body, she wrapped her strong arms around him to pull him to safety.

Medb fought her way to their position. Seeing Ysbaddaden lying on his side, his teeth clenched, she couldn't make her legs hold her up. She felt such a passionate anguish, it shocked her. As she dropped beside him, she saw his face was ashen beneath his chestnut beard. His tunic was slashed across his back, the edges of the cut soaked with bright red blood. Lifting the edges of that sodden cloth, she found an open, painful-looking axe slice that laid bare several of his ribs. It would have brought any other man his end, but Ysbaddaden still breathed.

Skatha hurriedly unbuckled his mail. "Help me!" she shouted at Medb.

Stung into motion, Medb drew Ysbaddaden's undervest of leather off him and set it aside with the mail coat. Old scars crisscrossed his torso, chiefly on the right side of his body. Blood gushed from the new wound. Skatha shook her head as she accepted a rag from one of her soldiers and pressed it into the wound, trying to staunch the flow.

"Why did you do that?" Medb cried out. "You came within a breath of killing yourself!"

If he wasn't as good as dead already.

He didn't respond. He seemed beside himself with pain.

Medb stood, looking for her Druids. She found Ceridwen, shadowy, standing right amid a thorn thicket where nobody could have walked. And Diancecht stood atop a column of stone no man could have scaled. Already they were chanting. Ceridwen lifted her arms in an arc above her head; Diancecht did the same.

Ysbaddaden stiffened on the ground, his eyes screwed shut.

Of course they would heal him. Of course he would live. His unthinking high spirits, his pure physical vigor, would throb on through his veins. Anything else was impossible.

He relaxed as the healing spells let go of him, and coughed and opened his eyes. Faint color appeared in his face. The horrendous wound wasn't healed completely, and Medb knew the mages had no time to concentrate on that task at the moment, but he would not die.

Weak, and still in pain, he looked at Medb and spoke in a quiet, labored voice. "I'm sorry."

In those words, she knew that his iron determination had given way. Under other circumstances she might have seen it as a good thing. She might have welcomed it with joy and relief. Right now it only made her feel desperate. She needed all his strength of will today.

"Medb!"

She lifted her head at the sound of Balor's voice. "Do you still think you can win this battle?"

Skatha selflessly drew his attention to herself by standing and shouting, "Be gone, foul Balor, lord of carrion!"

He swiveled and opened his evil eye on her, and at the same time his drear, cold voice warned, "Come not between Balor and his prey."

Skatha shivered, and her eyes rolled up into her head.

Ysbaddaden, with Medb's help, rose to his feet. "Give me my shirt . . . my armor."

"You can't fight!"

He turned her a fierce look. "I can fight–but only you can win this day." He took her face between his hands. "It rests with you, Medb."

It rests with you. That is what her father had said.

Why her? Why?

She suddenly knew she could do many things, but she couldn't kill Balor with the Gae Bolga. She shook her head. "I can't. I should have given you the Gae Bolga from the start."

"And I shouldn't have been so reckless that now I can't help you. But Skatha can throw it. Give it to her. We'll clear the way for her."

Medb gave him a doubting look.

"You've always been wiser than me, so be wise now. Give the spear to Skatha."

At length, she nodded sharply. She reached to sling the spear off her back and held it out to her old teacher. "You must be our *cearbhallain*, our spear thrower, our victor."

Skatha looked at the weapon soberly. "I don't know, that last blast . . . I feel as empty as an old pail." Yet she took it, and the spear seemed to give her new strength. She had been drooping before; now she stood straight. "It should have been Ysbaddaden."

"But I have been a fool," he said.

Skatha nodded. "I'll do my best."

"We can ask no more of you," Medb said.

As the three of them turned back to the battle, they found that Tristan and Diancecht had weakened the Fomors guarding Balor. Ribbons of drool hung from the beasts' mouths. Yet, the combined assault had cost Medb's spellcasters as well. Ceridwen especially seemed exhausted. They needed rest to restore their vitality. No matter, they had done their jobs, and so had Llud, on the other side of the marshes. Medb and Ysbaddaden attacked with renewed determination. Ysbaddaden spared himself not at all. He pressed the enemy as no one else could have done with such a wound as he had.

Fewer were they, but they cleaved through the Fomors like a fire flash in the forest. And finally no more brutes stood between them and the King of All Monsters.

Critically weakened, Balor stumbled, and pulled off his horned helmet, as if it were suddenly too heavy for his shoulders to support. Even his evil eye employed less destruction as it opened on Medb. He didn't seem to see Skatha step forward and aim the

Gae Bolga. As she made the necessary run to launch it, she couldn't contain her effort in silence. A great cry rose out of her as she loosed the deadly spear.

Balor's protected position suddenly became his prison of death. He had nowhere to go, no place to hide from the many-barbed spear. He gave a terrific bellow as he saw the weapon hurling toward him. Yet Medb saw no horror, no protest in his face. Only surprise. His last sensation on this earth was astonishment that Fate had found the temerity to thwart him at last.

His bellow became a screech as the Gae Bolga buried itself in his evil eyeball. Skatha had launched it with such force that it came out at the back of his head. Its shaft shivered. Medb ducked down and cowered, as did everyone else, and a wise thing, since the Fomor seemed to burst inward on himself. Great flashes of light radiated out from him, then were sucked in again, as the diabolical powers and demonic energies that the beast had controlled struggled to survive his death and failed.

Balor fell, and the impact of his body seemed to shake the very roots of his island. The ground beneath Medb's feet rumbled. A fissure opened up almost at her toes, and ran out from there, widening, until it broke open directly beneath Balor. The dark lord fell through, into the earth, and disappeared.

But the rumbling didn't stop. Other fissures opened, and great landslides of rocks began to roll down the peaks. Ceridwen screamed, "The island is going under!"

Suddenly the pandemonium of battle became the bedlam of chaos. Medb shouted, "To the boats!"

The remaining Fomors staggered on their thick legs. Clever Bress said, "Save yourselves, fools!" But they didn't know how they should do that.

Medb led Skatha and Ysbaddaden down the slipping, sliding shore as her flotilla of boats tried to come in. She shouted at her armies, "Discard your armor and weapons! We must swim for the boats!"

Ten, then twenty, then a hundred soldiers plunged into the churning waves, the boats their only hope as the island shook them off as a dog shakes off a drenching.

Medb and Skatha stayed close to Ysbaddaden, fearing he might not make it. At the first boat, sailors held out their oars for them to grab. They were pulled in, and forgotten as the sailors turned to pull in others.

Medb found a cloak in which to wrap Ysbaddaden, who was shivering, all his will to survive failing him now that Balor was dead. Once she'd seen he was as comfortable as could be, she turned to help the sailors save her escaping army.

She paused as the peak of the tallest crag of the island cracked and wobbled and finally fell. At the same time, the captain of her boat gave his rowers the order to back off from the island. Medb scanned the churning sea to make sure that the last few of her soldiers made it aboard other boats. All that was left in the water were those few Fomors with the sense to abandon their disintegrating stronghold. Four of these, commanded by evil Clach grabbed at the working oars of Medb's boat. As the sailors struggled to pull their oars free, exhausted soldiers sprang to the bulwarks to jab at the paddling beasts. "Be gone!" "Drown, you rotten wretches!" "Go down with your demon master and his evil island!"

For Tory Island was going down, sinking under the sucking waves, even as Medb watched. Had Balor's control of the dark forces alone lifted it out of the sea? Perhaps so.

As the oarsmen worked to escape the suction created by its sinking, Medb, with Skatha at her side, stared as the last of the drear outpost slipped beneath the tide.

Shortly after the conquering army arrived safely home, the horns of peace sounded. They blared from the northern shores of Omagh to the wooded hills of Cobh in the far, fair south; from isolated Aran Isle to grand Kilcullen. The shadows had been driven abroad, Queen Medb had won her kingdom, and Eire had survived. Celebrations shimmered with light and many a jovial hour of mischief and play occurred during that snowy Samhain following Balor's death. And in time, the true magnitude of what the Evil Eye's death meant, the profound inner realization that they were free, sank into the hearts and minds of the Tuatha de Dannan.

The snows melted, and Imbolc came booming in on a high wind so light-filled that the new grass glistened and tinkled like green crystal. Light entered each new day as it did the diamond Lia Fail, striking every surface at an angle, reflecting back from it, and spreading out its colors brilliantly. All unhappiness, all discontent gave way to the calmer, simpler pleasure of knowing what each new morn would bring. In their gratitude, the folk of Eire promised their Goddess that they would be better than they had been before, for they were a new people happy to be alive.

As for Medb, praises would be sung in her name for years to come. She had many duties to attend to during that winter. While Ysbaddaden went to Ben Skellig with Skatha to recover from his savage battle wound, Medb was feasted night after night wherever she traveled. Yet the first greening of the land found her at home at last.

Connaught, her birthplace, her refuge. She went abroad on the soil of her forebears with exquisite sensitivity to each detail. After her small, brief dance in the flames of fate, it was as if her eyes had been widened, her ears opened, her nose cleared. She noticed the rainbow after the rain as if for the first time, and felt the suppleness of each thread in the weave of Ehtne's loom work. She saw the fluidity and expertise of her plowmen, and breathed in the dark ambrosia of the newly turned earth. One night, she and Fann went out onto the palisades of

Seamaire and raised their heads to the heavens milky with stars. Medb would hold out her bare hands as if to a warm rain, wonder-struck at the diamond-studded improbability of night without the accompaniment of dread.

She fell in love again that year, with life.

For some weeks she merely rested. She had believed, all through her ascension to power, that to live quietly again was all she wanted. But now she was surprised to discover that she'd become accustomed to being active, to making plans, even to running risks. Gwawl had told her to live, and to do that she discovered she must have bustle, music, the flaring light of candles and brands, the noise of people coming and going, laughing, talking, arguing gay and desperate ventures. And so one evening in mid-spring she called her council together at a table placed under the eaves of the forest. They enjoyed a meal in the open air, then, over cups of good ale, she shared with them her plans for the future of Eire.

"I want to send out envoys to all the provinces, requesting quarterly reports. And we should inform the chieftains that henceforth there will be an annual congress, after the harvests of Llughnasad are in. We will hold it here this year, and after that, we'll rotate the honor of hosting it so that each province takes its turn."

Matth slapped the table. "Thunder and fire, what a remarkable idea, my Lady!"

She looked sideways at Tochmarc and found him

beaming at her. He looked rested and carefree and almost young again in that soft dusk. Li Ban, too, smiled. She'd been doing that more often lately. It relieved Medb to see her recovering from her grief. In fact, she'd recently shown great interest in updating her maps, and a good thing, for Medb was going to need a complete knowledge of her domain.

One morning shortly thereafter, very early it was, a visitor rode through the stone arch of the citadel. Who it was Medb didn't know, for she could get nothing out of Li Ban when she questioned her. Therefore it was without forewarning that Ainle, who stood guard at the door of her hall, passed Ysbaddaden in.

The warrior paused just inside the threshold, looking at Medb for all the world as if she struck him breathless. She half rose from her throne, then sat again, gripping its arms at the sight of his smile and his broad shoulders.

I shouldn't be so glad to see him. Oh, Danu, don't make me care for him again. He's too reckless, too bent on his own way, too much altogether for me.

It was no good, for Ysbaddaden was there, very much alive, flinging off his cloak and striding across to her. Something she'd kept tightly lashed down tore free inside her and rushed to meet him.

He wore a plaid tunic of red and ginger, and ginger leggings that encased his powerful legs. He looked full of health, his skin gleaming copper-gold in the firelight.

"I'm glad to see you recovered, my friend."

"And I'm glad to see you so comfortable on your throne, princess."

She ignored the familiarity and the sensation of pleasure it gave her. "You've traveled far. The journey from Ben Skellig is no simple jaunt, as I recall. But perhaps you've taken up the life of a wanderer again and don't mind the travails of the road?"

"No more wandering for me. I've found my home."

She nodded. He had always liked Ben Skellig, and Skatha would be glad to count him among her champions. "Why have you come to Connaught?"

"Don't you know?" Because of the way he leaned near her, because of the look in his eyes, for a long moment everything hung shining.

He broke the spell by straightening away. "For one thing, I came to thank you for preserving me from my own foolishness on Tory Island. I was as stupid as a barrel of bristles that day. I knew I was the most accomplished at throwing the Gae Bolga, but instead of trusting you to see that in the end, I rushed forward and nearly got myself killed. I thank you for saving me."

"It wasn't me alone. Skatha, and Ceridwen, and–"

"Yes," he gestured the names away. "I owe them all my thanks. But I begin–and end–with you."

She accepted his thanks with a grave and stately nod. What did he mean, though, begin and end with her?

He glanced about the hall. "Can we not go out into the good sunshine to talk?"

Leaving the citadel on horseback, Medb nodded to Roc, who as captain of her guard stood watch at the main gate. The farm folk were in the fields, or working in the blue morning shadows about their lodges. Without thinking, Medb took Ysbaddaden to her headland, where she never took anyone. They had to cross hedges and streams, and a crooked bit of bog, but then they rode through the great woods that endured for miles around, and nearing the spot, left their horses and climbed to the very height of the cliff's edge.

For several moments, they both stood struck silent with awe. The sunlight poured over them like melted butter. The sea glistened. The marvel of it all, that she was home, that the days of fear were passed, overcame her.

Striving for lightness, she laughed, "You won't push me over the edge this time, I hope."

He didn't answer, and she turned to look up at him. The light struck sparks of russet and gold in his hair, and gilded his tanned face, and showed the depths of his level brown eyes. He smiled, but she saw that there was something he wanted to say. At length, he made an attempt to voice it.

"Ceridwen visited me in Ben Skellig. She told me that the beginning of wisdom comes when a man realizes the world doesn't turn on him." His expression displayed how hard this was for him. "That day when I put myself in harm's way–when I thought I might die and never see this freedom we've won–I came to a turning point. I think perhaps I gained the door to wisdom."

He took in a great breath, and seemed to shed his reflective mood, which would always be more foreign to him than outright action. "Gained it, though I'm not sure I've stepped over the threshold yet. But anyway . . ." he shrugged, and looked back at the land, "I've decided that I should be content to call this place home–if you will allow me."

Without knowing she spoke, Medb exclaimed quietly. Her heart hammered. She had a heady feeling, a sense of dancing on the edge of a void. Nonetheless, she managed a skeptical tone. "Does the din of the world bear no more appeal?"

"From what I hear, there's to be more than enough of the world coming and going around here to satisfy even me. But between times, I do believe I would live here happily. Of course, I shall always be ready to obey your able instructions and be your most humble servant, gentle and sweet-tempered to the last." He gave her a sidelong glance, one brow lifted.

Medb laughed outright. What else could she do, with this splendid figure beside her, filling the keen air with an absurd vow of obedience?

He laughed too, knowing that she, more than any other person, knew exactly what he was likely to do the first time he disagreed with anything she ordered. "All right, perhaps I'll always be arrogant and headstrong, but my intentions are good at this moment. And when it comes to battle, you know I'm a gnashing beast. I'm sure that should be of use to my Lady High Ruler now and again."

Medb laughed. "I missed you so after I left Ben Skellig. There was so much to do, so much to rebuild, and not an hour passed that I didn't wish you were here to help me."

Just for a moment the dark clang and clangor of those thick-piled years resounded in her soul. It was a feeling as though she might fall endlessly down through all the fear once more, and never hit bottom.

She shook off the sensation, and tried to return the conversation to its former cheerfulness. "So, I shall have a new home champion. Danu is good. We have the chance to build a far greater and happier Eire than ever before."

He nodded. "May She who makes harmony in heaven make harmony on Earth."

"And may we die abed years hence."

"Aye, when you're a skinny old woman and I'm a stooped old man, neither of us good for anything in this world anymore."

Medb's laugh covered a stab of pain, for she saw herself growing old alone, never experiencing the love Gwawl and Li Ban had shared. She didn't dare look at Ysbaddaden, for fear he would see her anguish. Blinking rapidly, she tried to think of something more to say.

No use. He took her chin to turn her face up to his. His expression had become very private, and he stared into her eyes as if to probe the soul behind them.

"What is it?" she asked.

"I am no good with words, you know."

She held her breath, for the moment demanded words. Nothing else would do.

"How does an ordinary warrior tell his Lady High Ruler that he would like to grow old with her, to share her every smile and feel her every sorrow in this life, and to abide with her even in the mystery beyond?"

The tears returned and flooded the eyes so fully exposed to him. This time she made no attempt to hide them. "You lie when you say you are no good with words. You wield them with as much magic as your sword."

"Are they as fateful as Answerer?"

She nodded slowly, and as slowly his mouth lowered to claim hers. A luminous spill of sensation filled her, a quiet surrender of the bones as Ysbaddaden gathered her into his arms. She seemed to hear Gwawl's voice: Live. She would, everlastingly. For it seemed unlikely that she and Ysbaddaden would ever grow old. They would be young forever. And beyond forever.

For death has no finality, and hope never dies.

NADINE CRENSHAW has won the prestigious Golden Heart Award given by the Romance Writers of America. She was also a finalist for the same group's Rita Award. Some of her previous titles include *Viking Gold* and *Destiny and Desire*.